FGTeeV
GAME BREAK!

HarperAlley is an imprint of HarperCollins Publishers.

FGTeeV: GAME BREAK!
Copyright © 2021 by Laffter Inc.
All rights reserved. Printed in the United States of America. No part of this book may
be used or reproduced in any manner whatsoever without written permission except in
the case of brief quotations embodied in critical articles and reviews. For information
address HarperCollins Children's Books, a division of HarperCollins Publishers,
195 Broadway, New York, NY 10007.
www.harperalley.com

ISBN 978-0-06-309298-3

Typography by Jessica Nordskog and Erica De Chavez
21 22 23 24 25 PC/WOR 10 9 8 7 6 5 4 3 2 1
❖
First Edition

Are you reading the copyright
page?! You must be a real FGTeeV
fan! True fans get a bonus activity.
Hidden throughout the book are
eleven teeny-tiny gurkey turkeys
for you to find. Good luck!

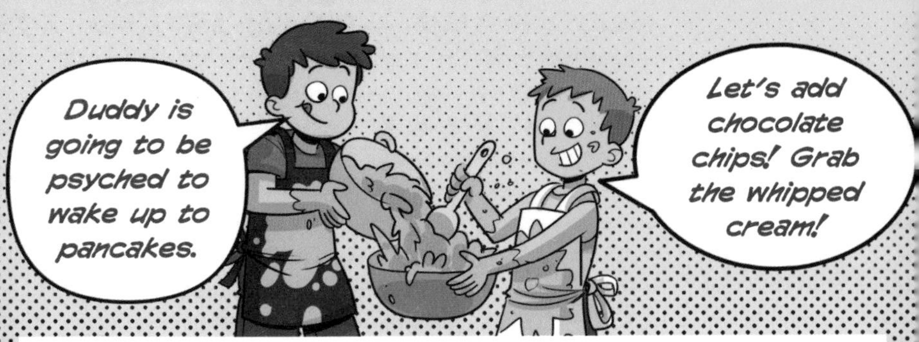
Duddy is going to be psyched to wake up to pancakes.
Let's add chocolate chips! Grab the whipped cream!

WHAT ELSE SHOULD THEY HAVE FOR BREAKFAST?

P	Q	V	B	S	Y	Z	R	G	P	R	X	N	W
W	A	D	J	G	B	P	J	O	K	Y	O	O	A
G	W	N	Q	G	M	N	A	F	H	C	M	X	F
D	N	X	C	E	K	T	L	O	A	N	X	H	F
H	U	Y	L	A	M	V	W	B	Q	W	X	I	L
H	B	C	O	E	K	K	Y	Q	Y	M	L	F	E
M	O	R	A	N	G	E	J	U	I	C	E	O	S
J	X	L	Z	M	K	A	S	O	V	B	B	V	N
V	L	W	W	R	L	S	B	Z	E	Y	J	W	J
E	K	S	U	U	B	P	V	U	F	S	Z	B	P
L	M	T	S	O	G	G	Z	D	P	H	B	O	J
E	F	Z	P	B	L	A	E	R	E	C	Z	P	L

TURKEY BACON ~~EGGS~~ CEREAL OATMEAL
ORANGE JUICE WAFFLES PANCAKES BAGEL

WHAT FOODS SHOULDN'T BE ON THE MENU?

Unscramble the words to find out!

yumgm rabes ____________ ____________

eheces labsl ____________ ____________

oht ucsea ________ ______________

kiplcse ____________

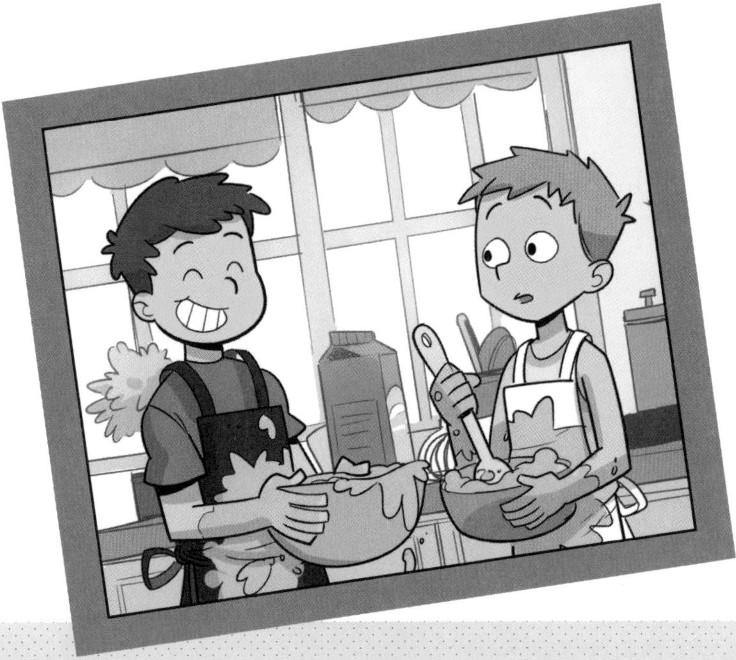

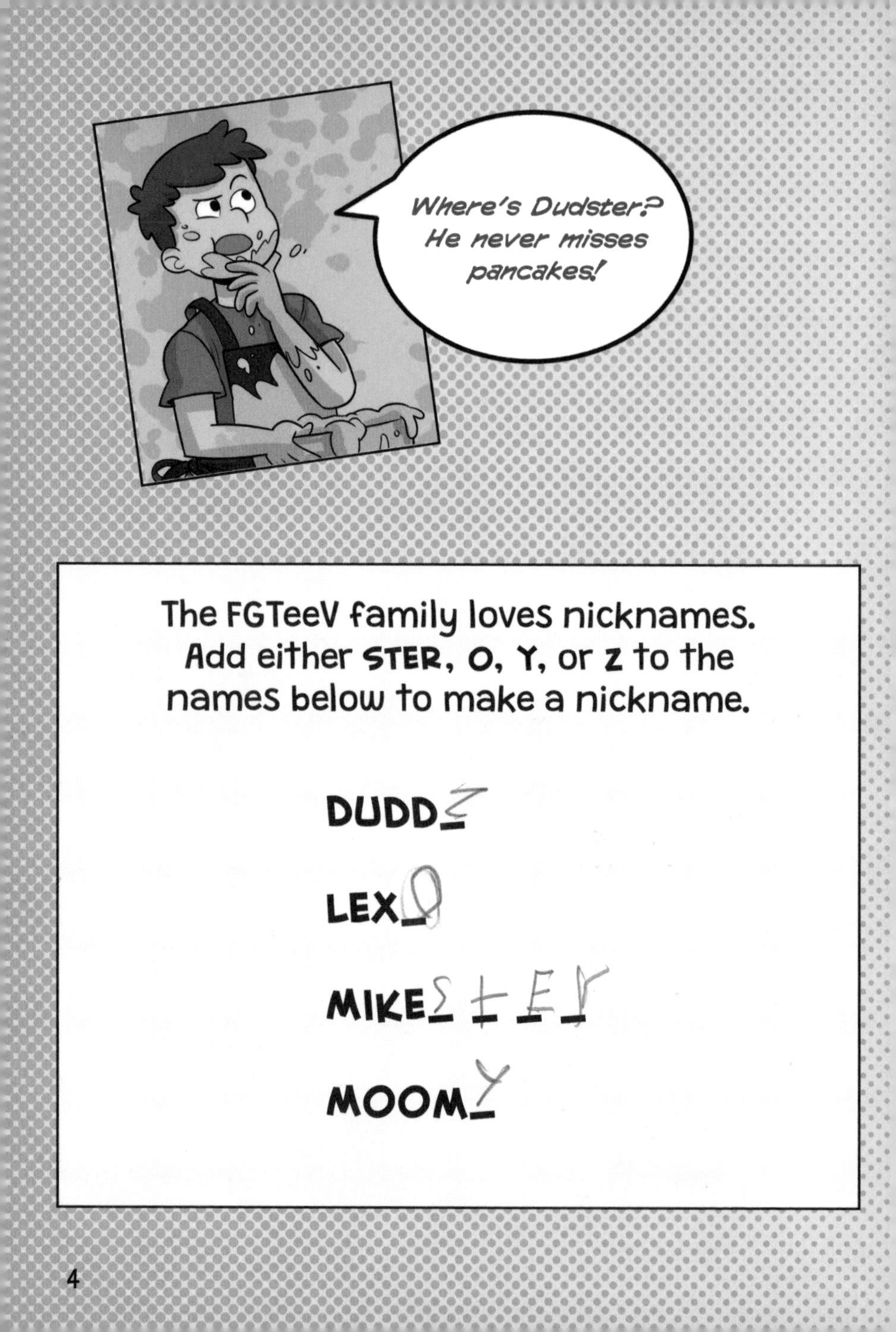
Where's Dudster? He never misses pancakes!

The FGTeeV family loves nicknames. Add either **STER**, **O**, **Y**, or **Z** to the names below to make a nickname.

DUDD_

LEX_

MIKE_

MOOM_

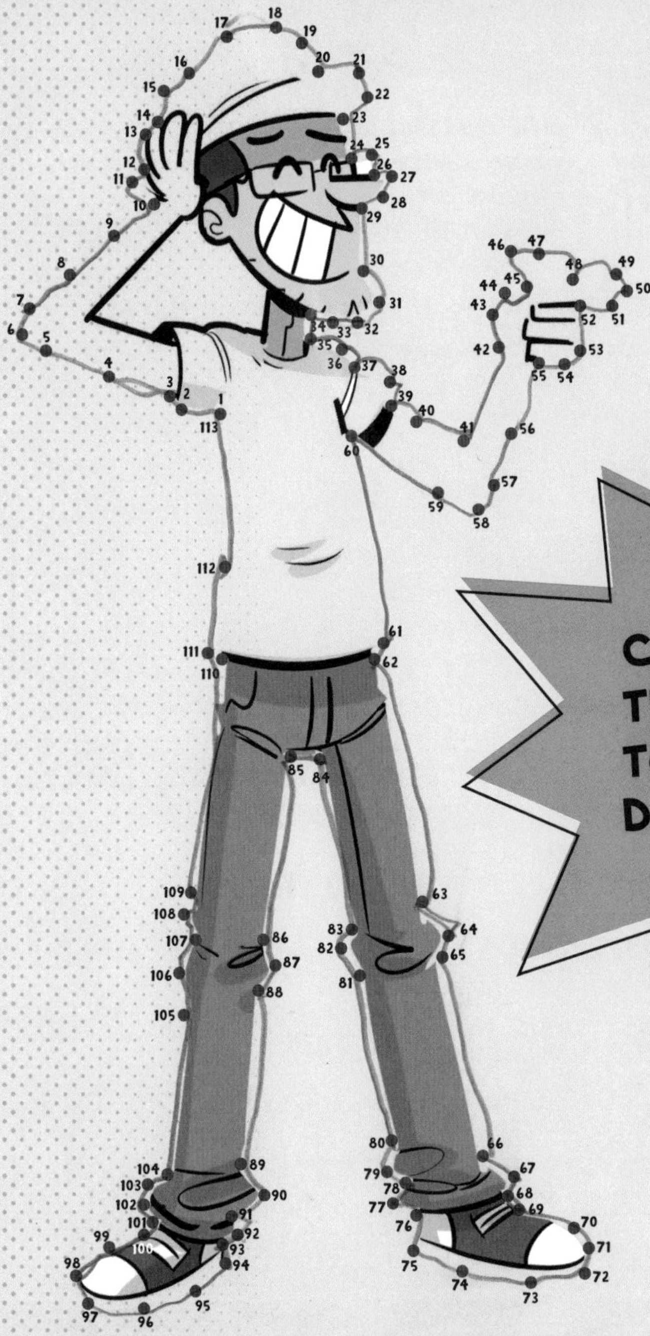

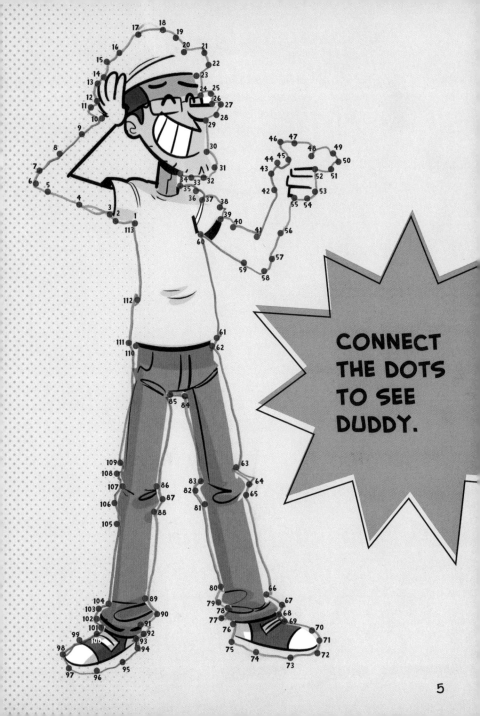

CONNECT THE DOTS TO SEE DUDDY.

Me and Duddz were up late last night playing Spookadilly Manor. That is one creepy game!
Circle the words that don't describe the house:
haunted
welcoming
safe
friendly
eerie

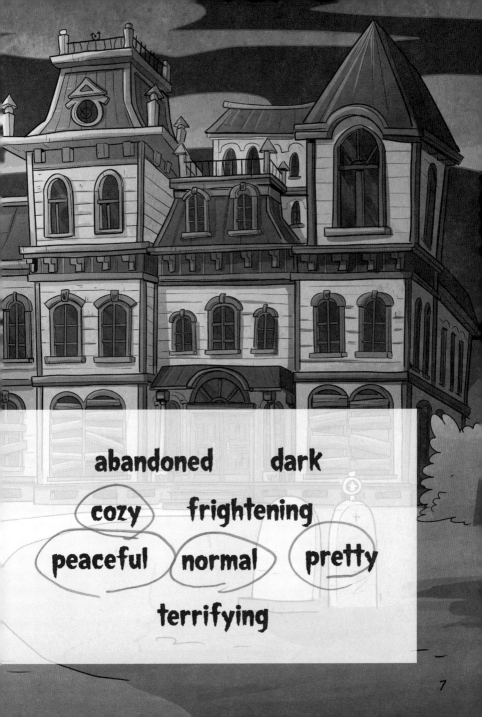

abandoned   dark

cozy   frightening

peaceful   normal   pretty

terrifying

7

SPOOKADILLY MANOR IS FILLED WITH GHOSTS.

Flip a coin to escape the haunted stairways.
Heads = move two spaces forward
Tails = move one space forward
Follow the instructions on the stair where you land. If it's blank, flip the coin again. Try to reach the finish line in as few coin flips as possible.

START

MOVE FORWARD ONE

MOVE BACK ONE

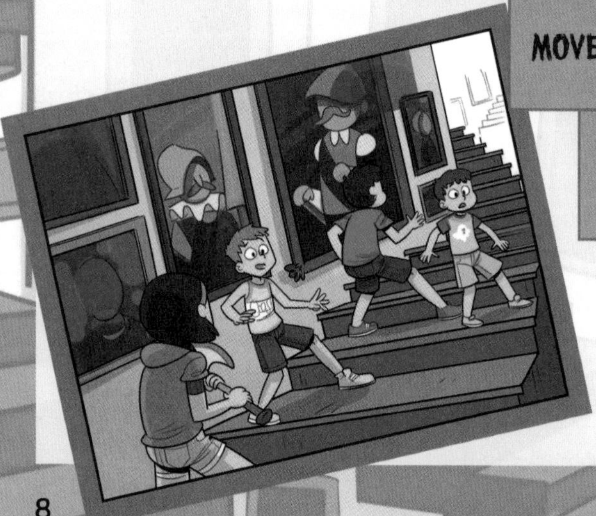

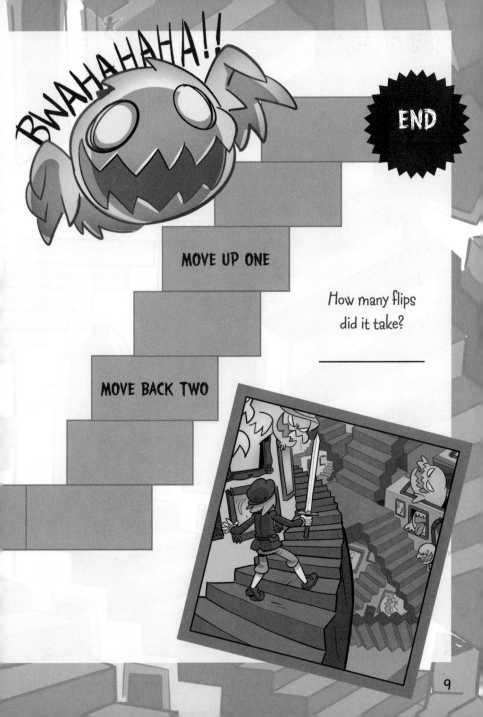

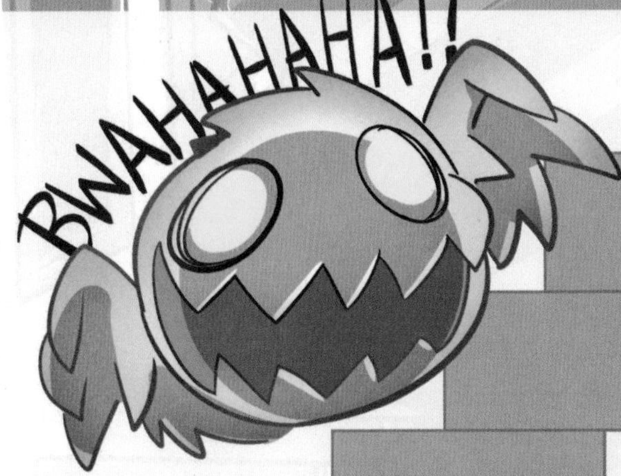
BWAHAHAHAHA!!

END

MOVE UP ONE

MOVE BACK TWO

How many flips
did it take?

____

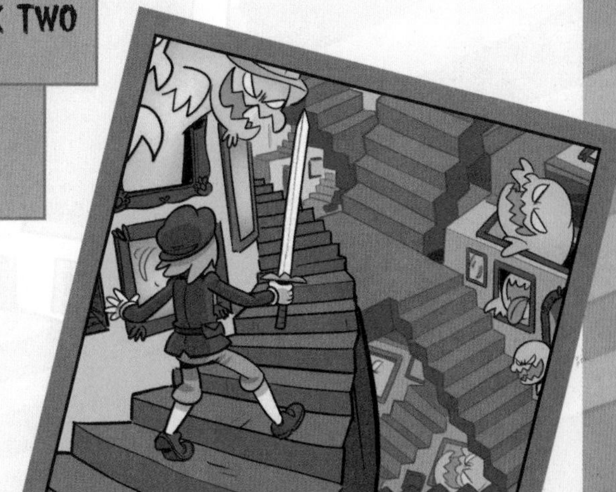

Try not to get lost in a haunted house—especially in the creepy basement!

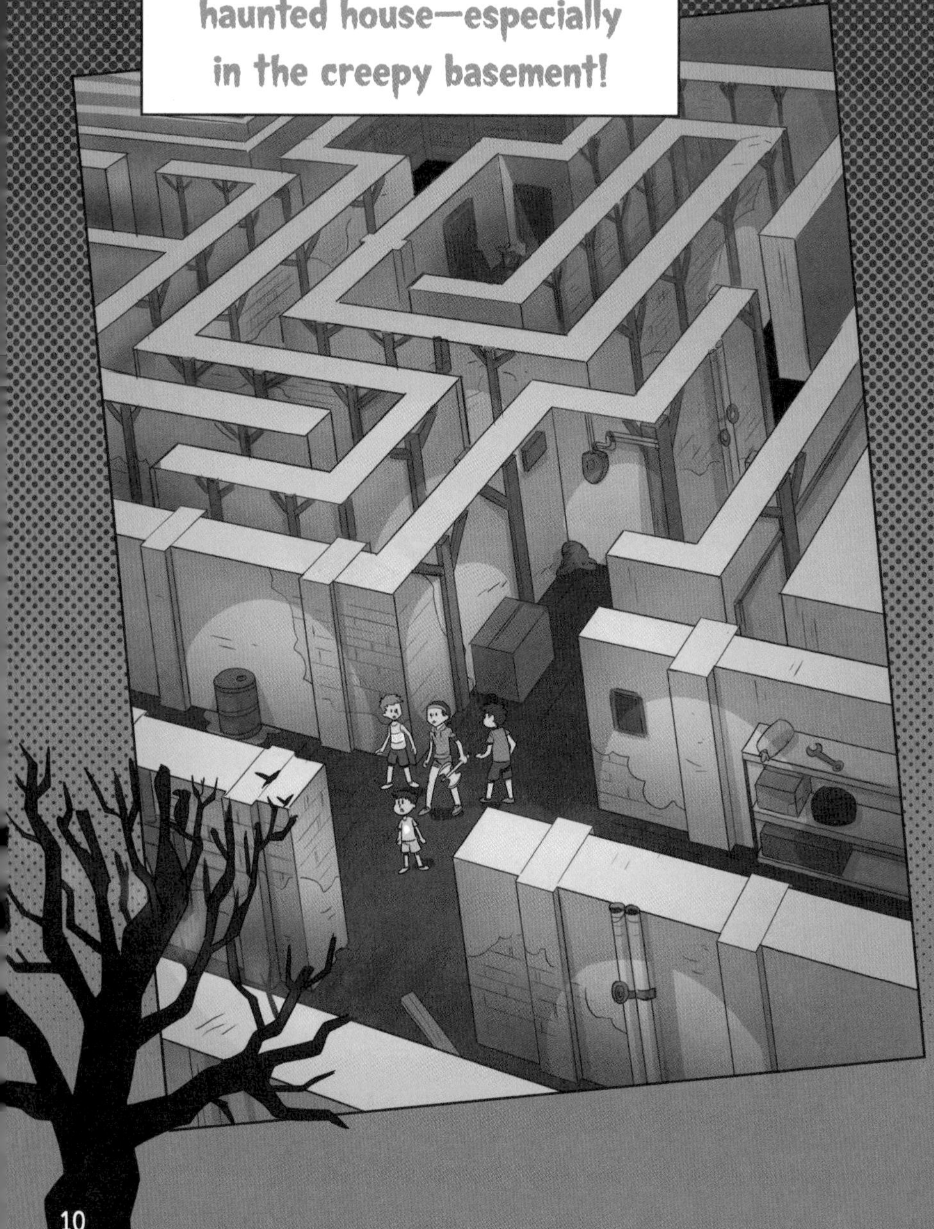

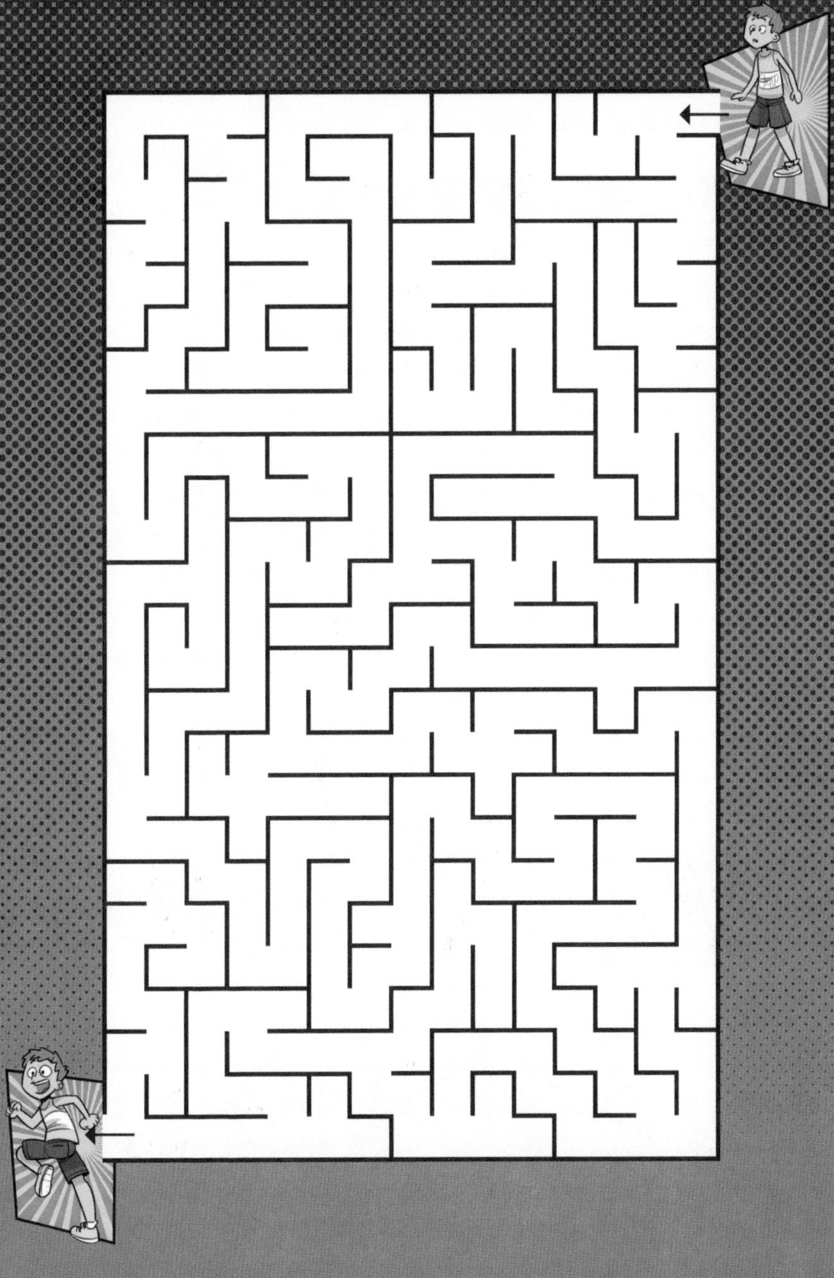

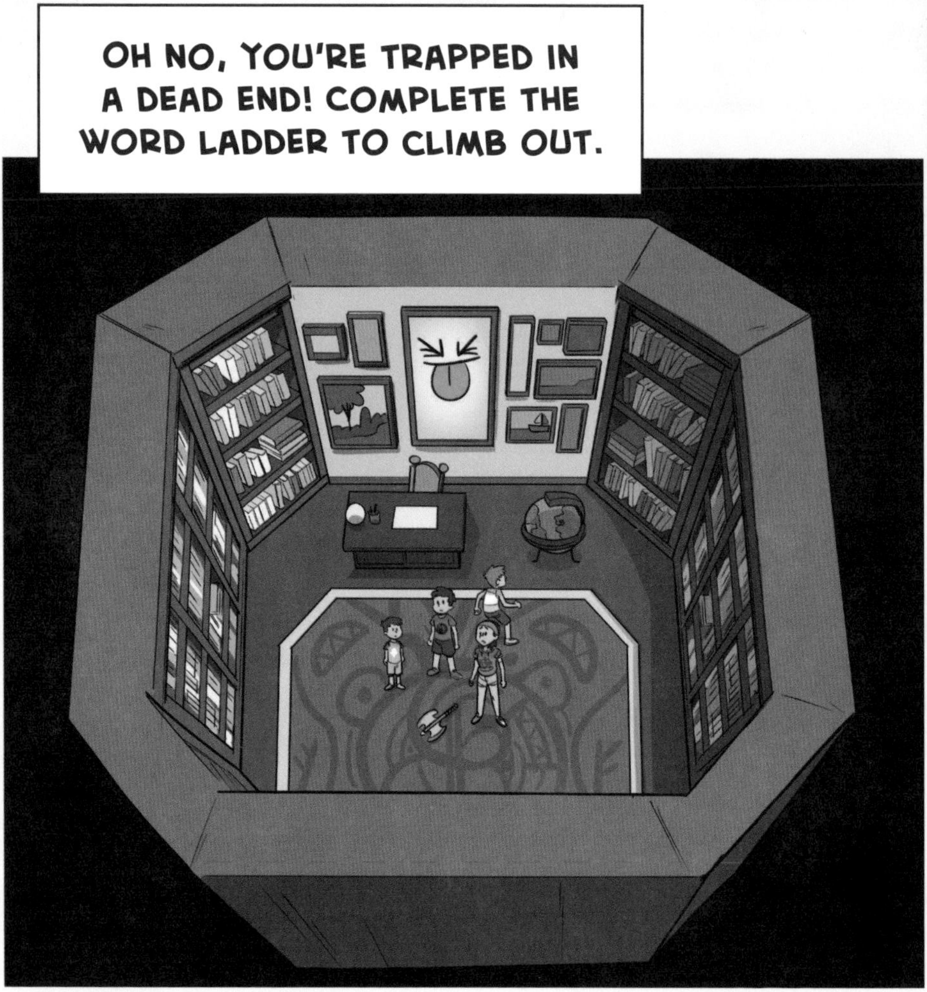
OH NO, YOU'RE TRAPPED IN A DEAD END! COMPLETE THE WORD LADDER TO CLIMB OUT.

Write a word that begins with an "a" on the first rung. On the second rung, write a word that begins with the second letter of your first word. And on the third rung, write a word that begins with the second letter of your second word, and so on until you reach the top.

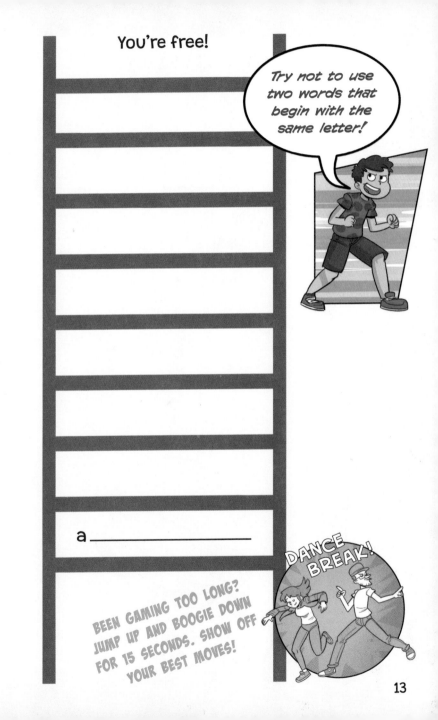

You’re free!

a ________________________

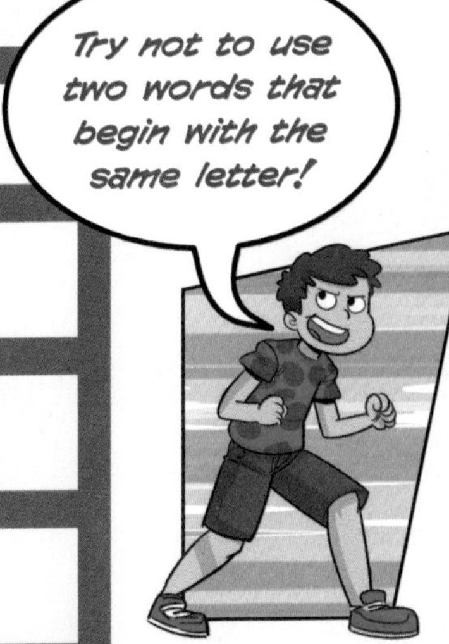
Try not to use two words that begin with the same letter!

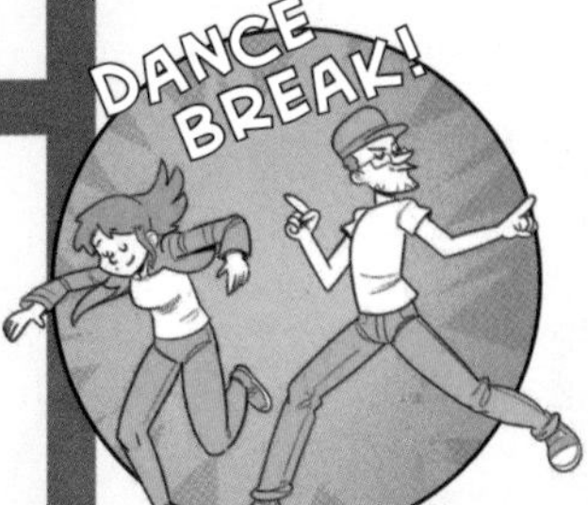
DANCE BREAK!

BEEN GAMING TOO LONG? JUMP UP AND BOOGIE DOWN FOR 15 SECONDS. SHOW OFF YOUR BEST MOVES!

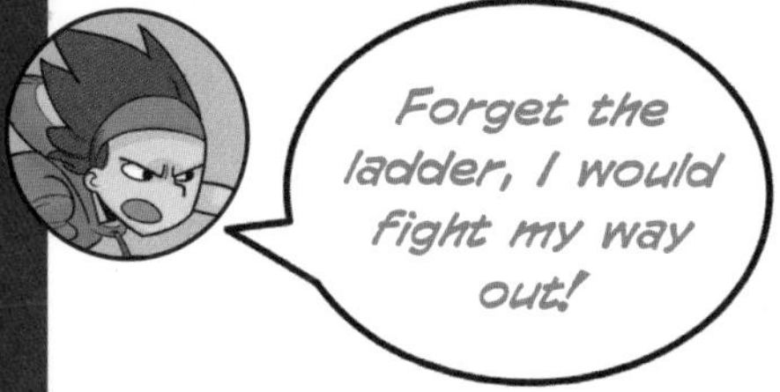
Forget the ladder, I would fight my way out!

Using the clues below, insert words into the blank spaces to see how Lexi would escape the dead end.

1. **Adjective**
2. **Body part**
3. **Piece of furniture**
4. **Noun**
5. **Name of a game**

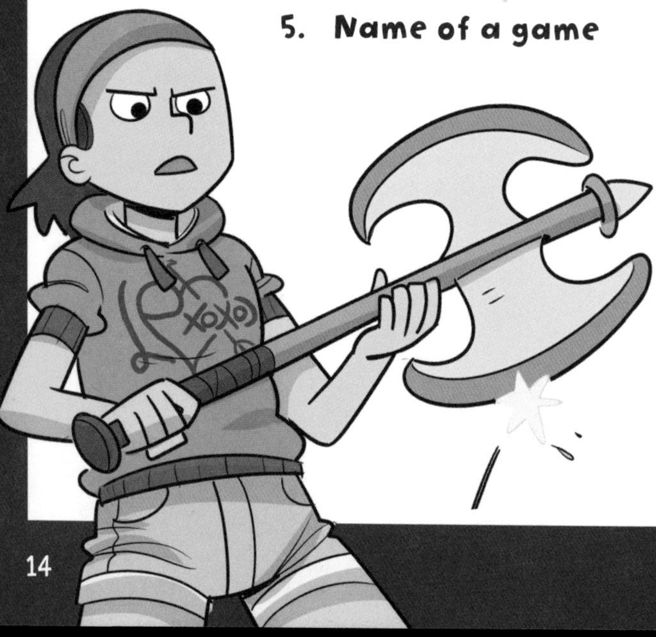
XOXO

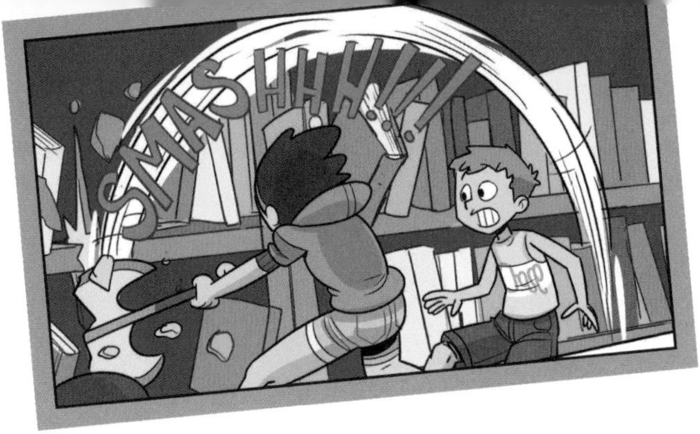
SMASHHHH!!

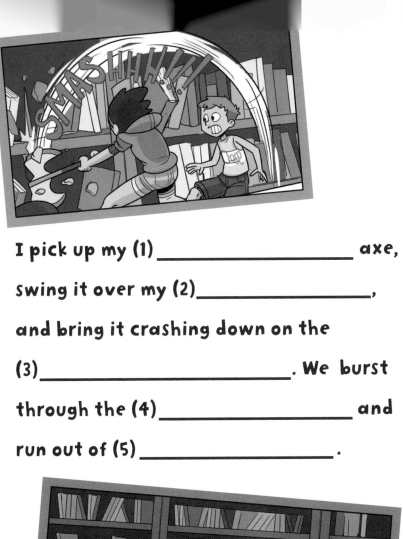

I pick up my (1) ____________________ axe,

swing it over my (2)____________________,

and bring it crashing down on the

(3)__________________________. We burst

through the (4)____________________ and

run out of (5) ____________________.

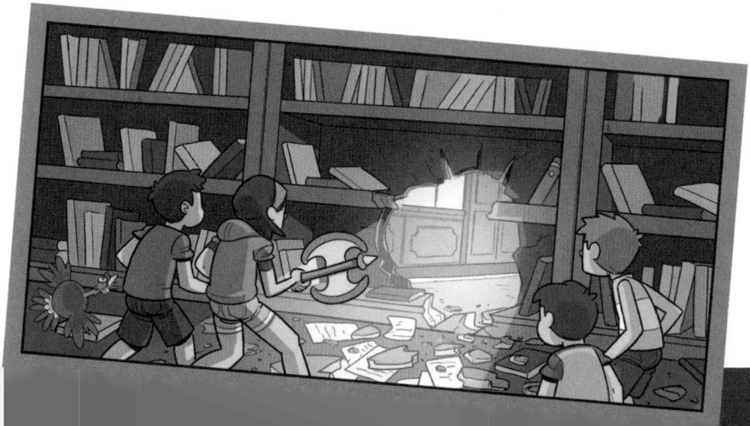

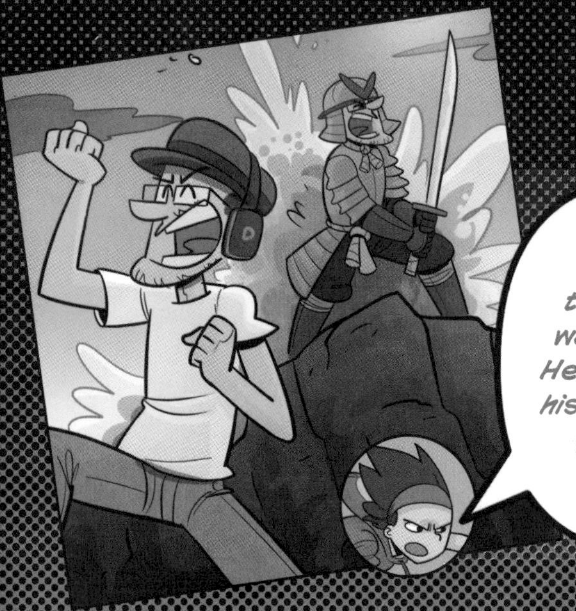
When I went to bed, Duddy was still playing. He wanted to use his sword to slice ghosts like a samurai.

FINISH THE CROSSWORD TO FIND OTHER WEAPONS HE COULD USE TO BATTLE GHOSTS.

ACROSS

1. Pointed tipped weapon with a long shaft you can thrust or throw
2. Huge gun that shoots explosive shells
3. Small bomb you throw

DOWN

3. Shoots bullets
4. Tool with handle and sharp steel blade
5. Sharp blade on a handle
6. Explosive device

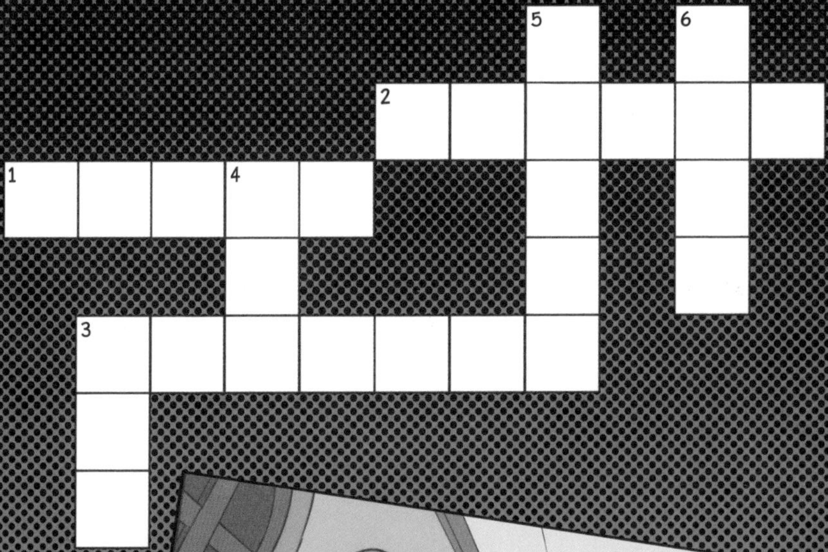

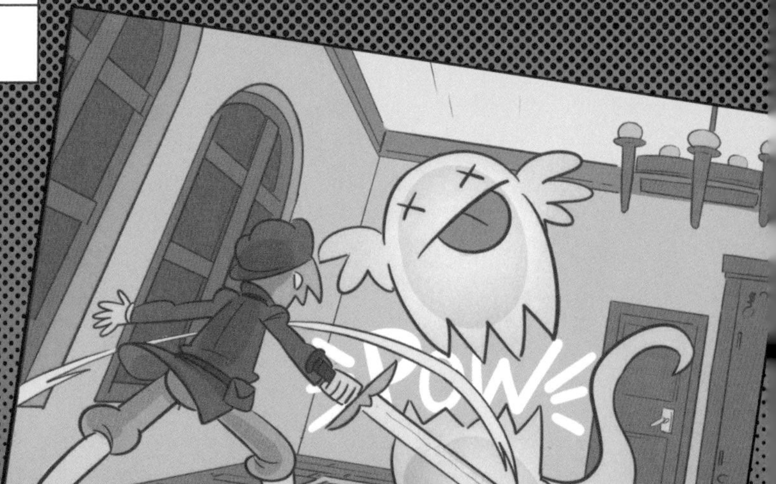
POW

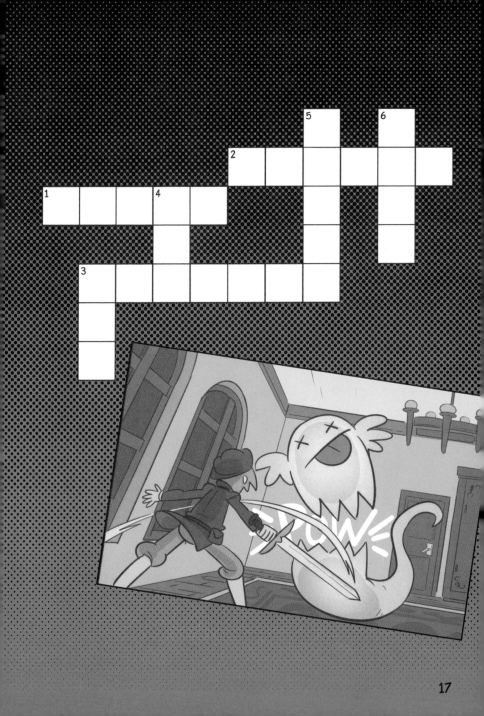

Maybe Duddz is out walking Oreo?

Which one is Oreo? She's one of the eight dogs shown that looks different. Circle her when you spot her!

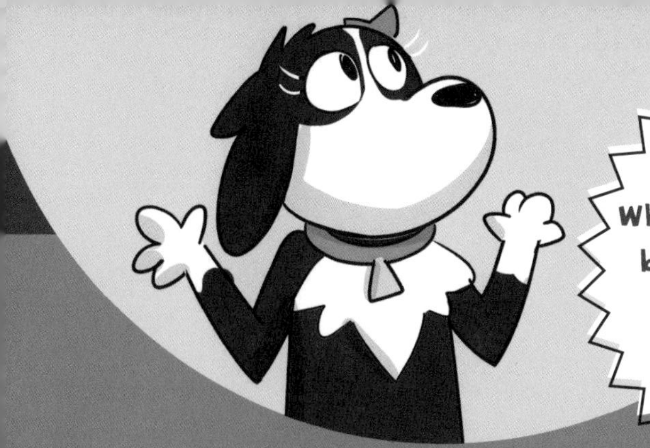

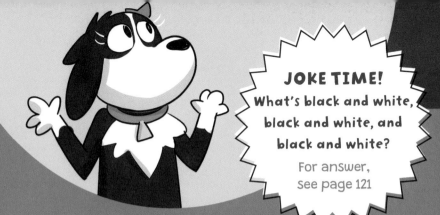

JOKE TIME!

What's black and white, black and white, and black and white?

For answer, see page 121

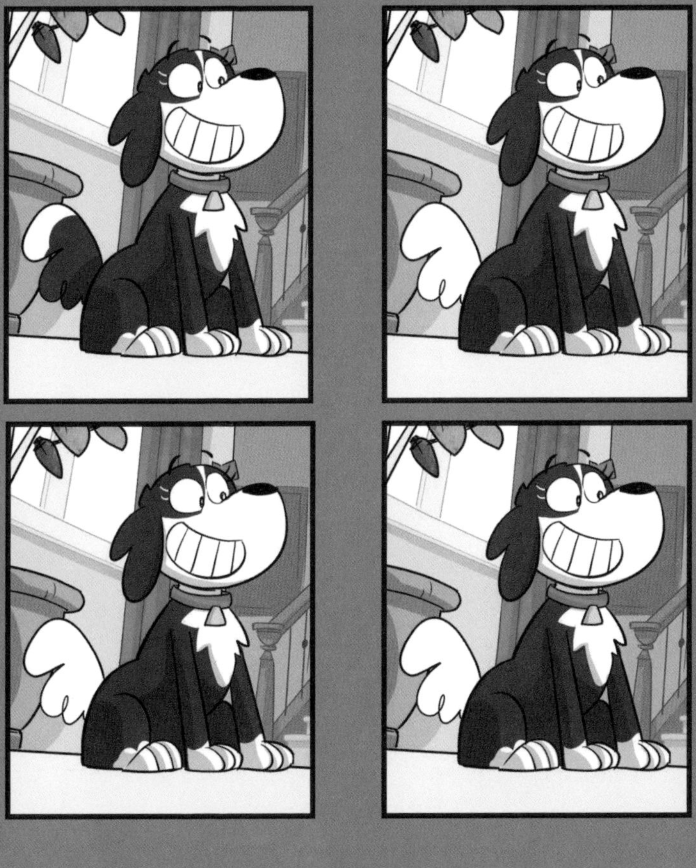

What if Oreo got off her leash? Duddy might be trying to catch her.

Help Oreo get to Duddy by drawing a line from each math problem to its correct answer.

Draw where you think Oreo could have gone.

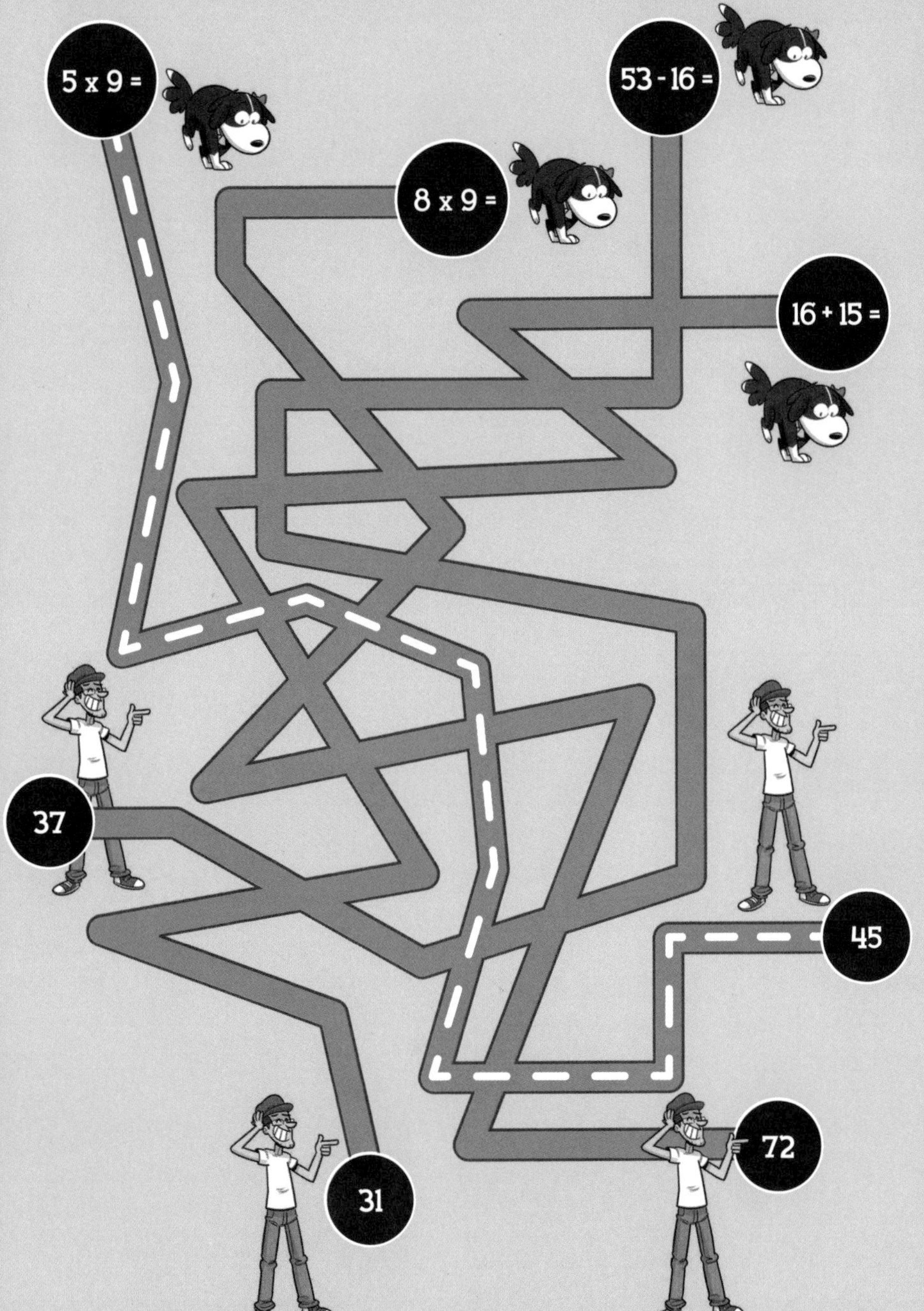
5 x 9 =
53 - 16 =
8 x 9 =
16 + 15 =
37
45
31
72

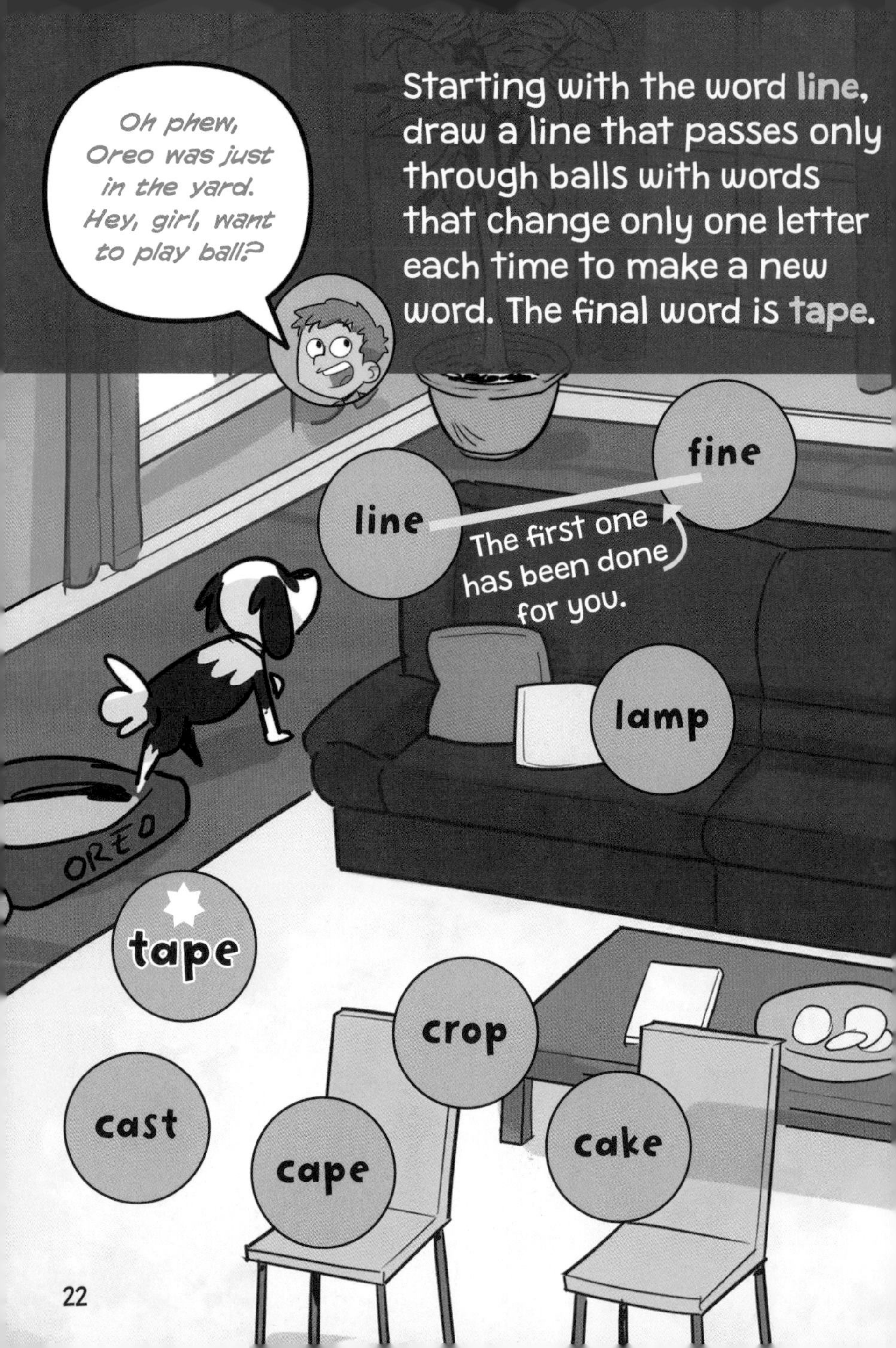
Oh phew, Oreo was just in the yard. Hey, girl, want to play ball?
Starting with the word line, draw a line that passes only through balls with words that change only one letter each time to make a new word. The final word is tape.
line
fine
The first one has been done for you.
lamp
ORE0
tape
crop
cast
cape
cake

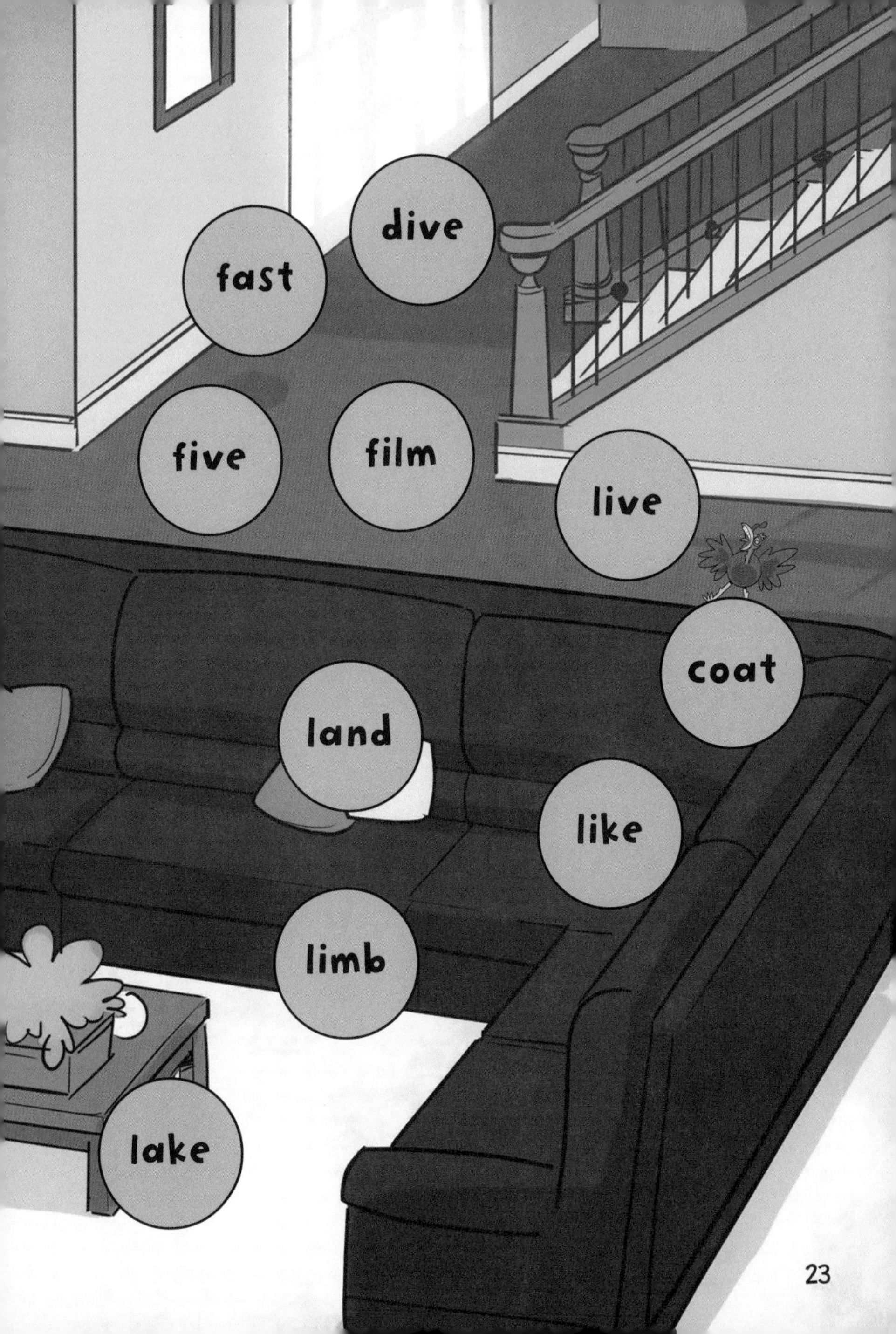
dive
fast
five
film
live
coat
land
like
limb
lake

WHAT DOES SHAWN SAY TO OREO WHEN HE GIVES HER A TREAT? USE THE KEY BELOW TO FIGURE IT OUT.

A = Z	N = M
B = Y	O = L
C = X	P = K
D = W	Q = J
E = V	R = I
F = U	S = H
G = T	T = G
H = S	U = F
I = R	V = E
J = Q	W = D
K = P	X = C
L = O	Y = B
M = N	Z = A

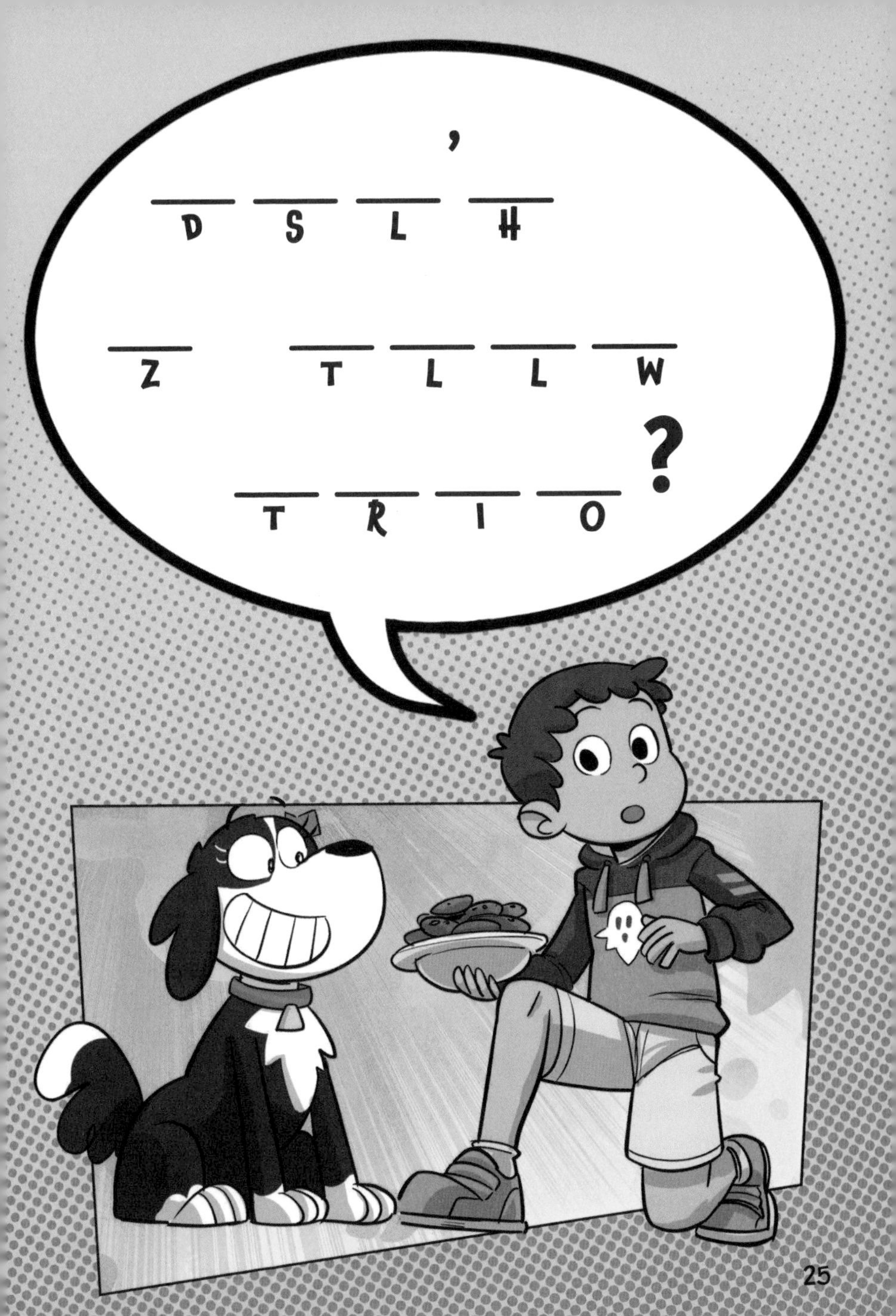
,
D S L H
Z T L L W
T R I O ?

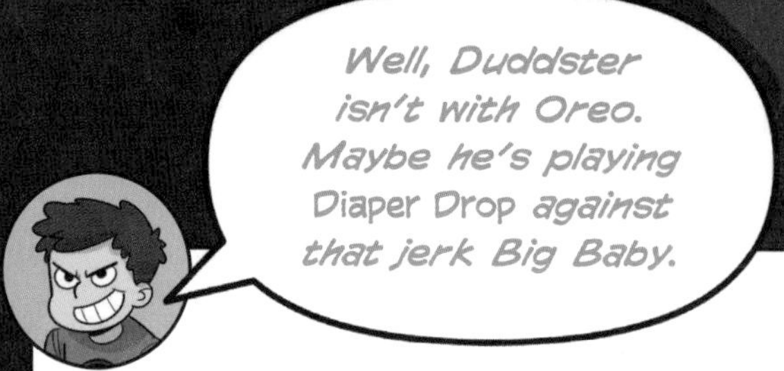
Well, Duddster isn't with Oreo. Maybe he's playing Diaper Drop against that jerk Big Baby.

Draw Big Baby's bottom half—
don't forget the stinky diaper!

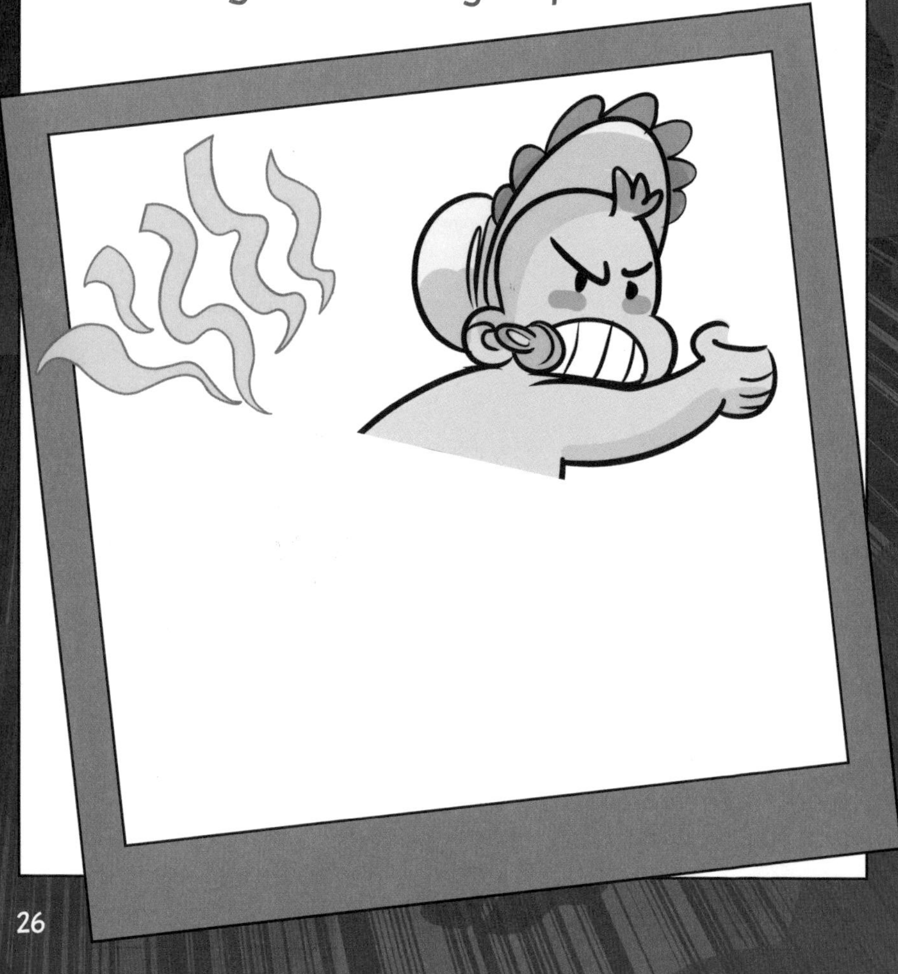

Big Baby's diaper isn't just stinky. Find and circle the words in the smelly search below.

```
V  I  P  N  Z  P  X  S  K  V  P  X  U  H
W  Z  D  B  R  P  K  I  W  U  F  F  O  C
G  R  D  I  S  G  U  S  T  I  N  G  D  Y
G  U  E  U  I  T  D  R  J  Z  U  M  O  T
S  G  W  T  T  X  I  G  J  D  F  X  R  R
M  S  N  E  C  D  N  E  T  T  O  R  O  I
G  E  O  P  S  H  K  T  Y  R  U  V  U  D
J  V  K  R  Y  D  E  D  S  M  Z  Z  S  J
D  O  T  T  G  R  R  D  Y  Y  K  T  X  S
L  A  S  H  B  X  Z  M  L  C  Z  B  G  E
C  A  P  Q  P  F  E  I  C  K  Y  I  A  I
N  B  U  C  M  M  D  Q  P  G  X  N  M  D
```

putrid	dirty	icky	rotten	bad
gross	nasty	odorous	wretched	disgusting

IN DIAPER DROP, YOU HAVE TO CLIMB A BUILDING TO SAVE BIG BABY.

Draw a line through the numbers with the greatest value on the scaffolding to get to the top.

BEEN GAMING TOO LONG? JUMP UP AND BOOGIE DOWN FOR 15 SECONDS. SHOW OFF YOUR BEST MOVES!

DANCE BREAK!

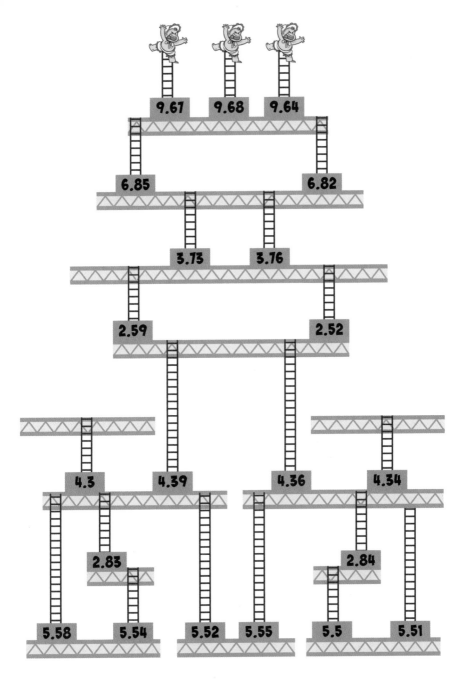

BIG BABY TRIES TO KNOCK YOU OFF THE BUILDING BY HITTING YOU WITH HIS POOP-FILLED DIAPER.

Circle what you'd rather be hit with than a stinky diaper:

pail of slop

 box of rocks

basket of hissing vipers

rotten eggs

feather pillow

Then draw a line to connect the missile and the name of a villain who would throw it at you:

box of rocks   Sooey Pig

hissing vipers   Caveman Carl

feather pillow   Lord Snake Pit

pail of slop   Cluck Cluck Buck

rotten eggs   Super Soft Sally

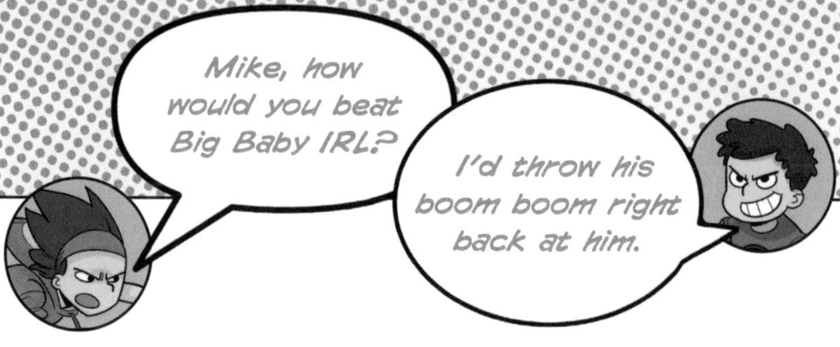
Mike, how would you beat Big Baby IRL?
I'd throw his boom boom right back at him.

Using the clues below, insert words into the blank spaces to see how Mike would defeat Big Baby.

1. Adjective
2. Noun
3. Something stinky
4. Favorite bad guy
5. Something tall

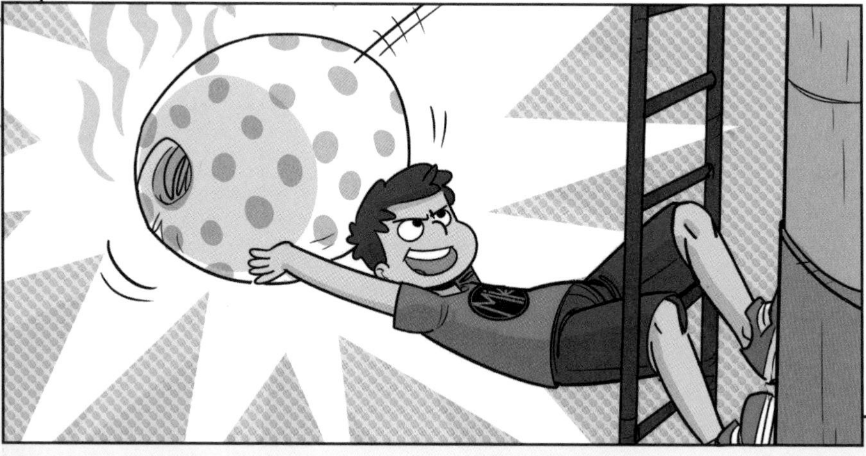

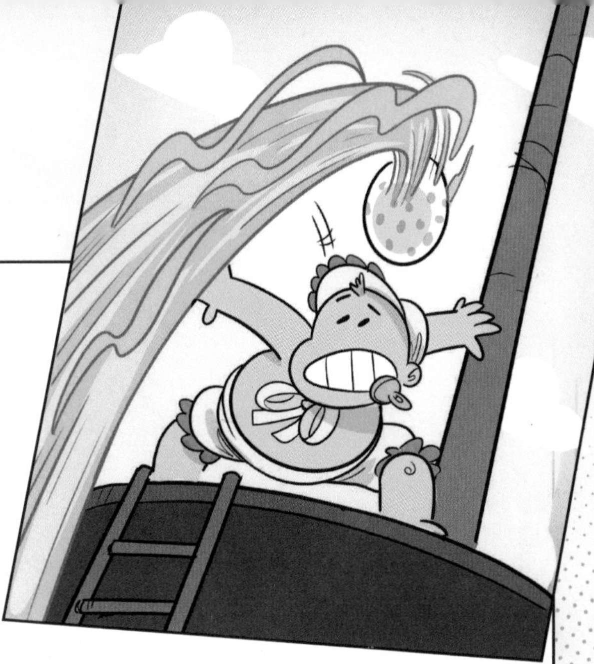

Mike climbs the (1) ______________ building,

holding tight to the (2) ______________ .

When Big Baby lets go with a giant

(3) ________________ , Mike catches it.

He whips it back at (4) ________________

____________, knocking him from the

(5) ______________ .

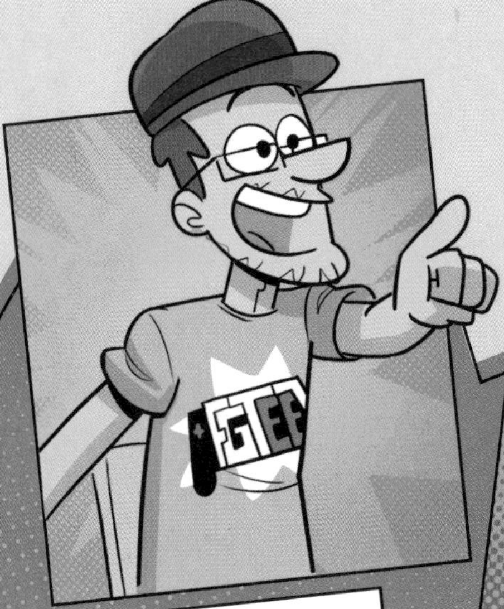

Duddy wears a shirt with the FGTeeV logo.

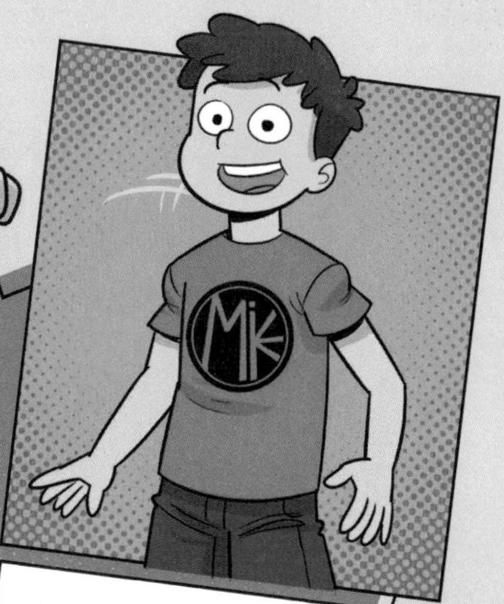

Mike's shirt has a cool design made out of his name.

CREATE A LOGO FOR YOUR NAME ON THE T-SHIRT ON THE FACING PAGE.

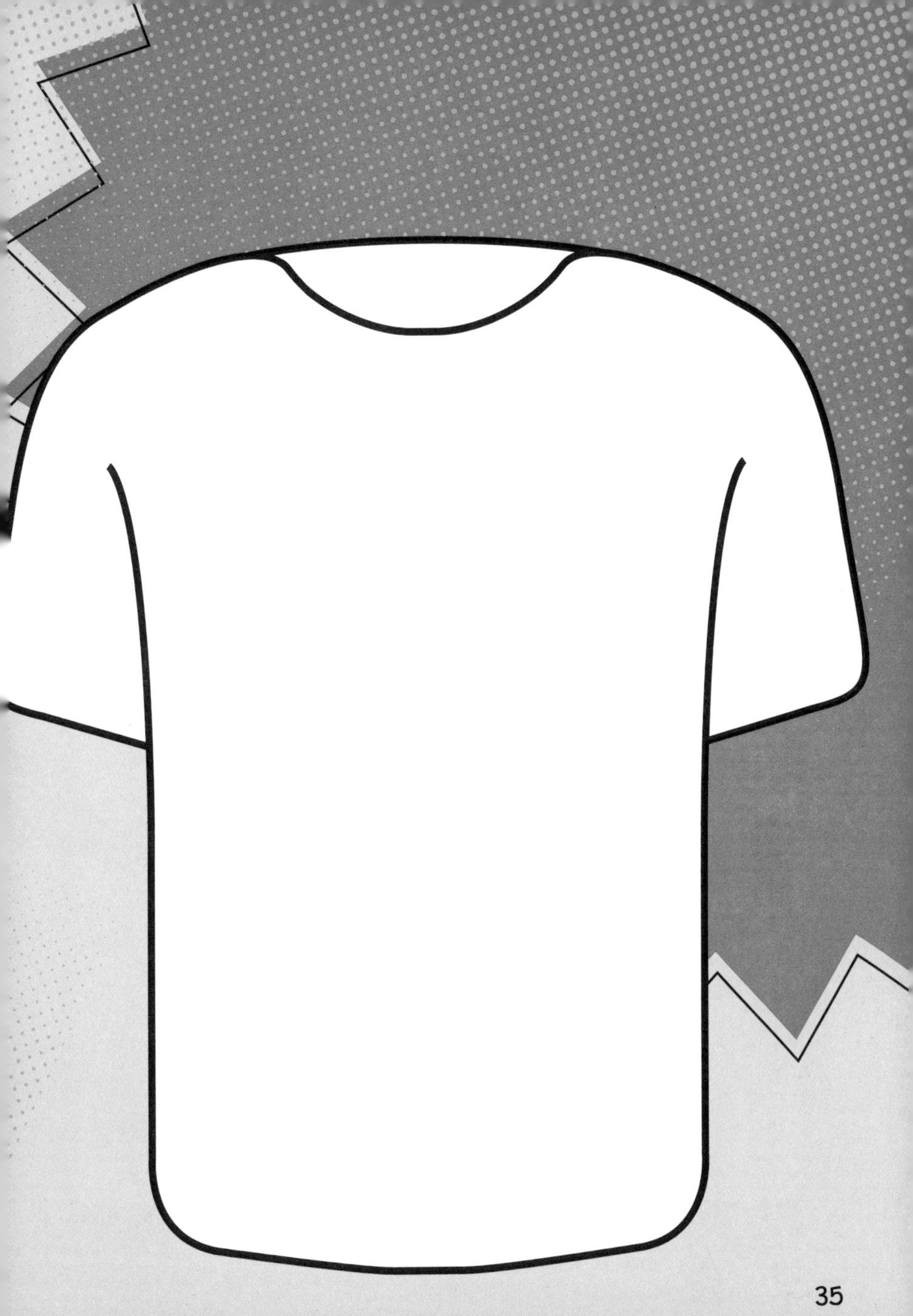

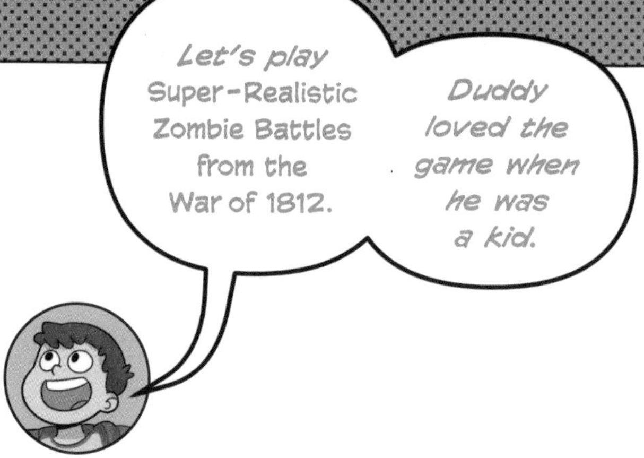
Let's play Super-Realistic Zombie Battles from the War of 1812.
Duddy loved the game when he was a kid.

Figure out the clues to fill in this **CORPSE-FILLED** crossword.

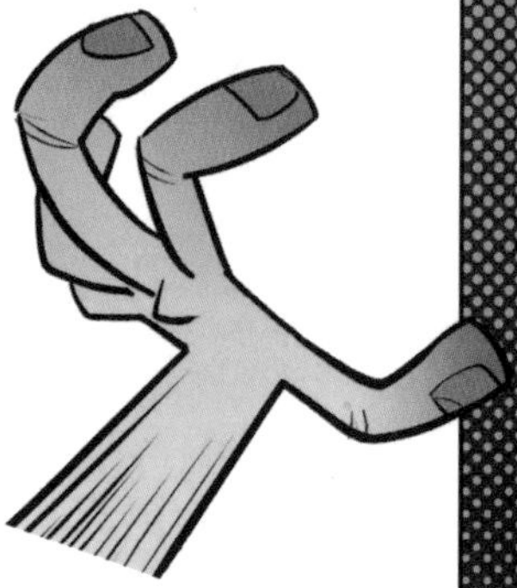

ACROSS

1. Dark time of day
2. Undead creature
4. What zombies eat

DOWN

3. When the dead suddenly rise and eat the living
5. What zombie mouths would do to your brains
6. Corpses that come back to life

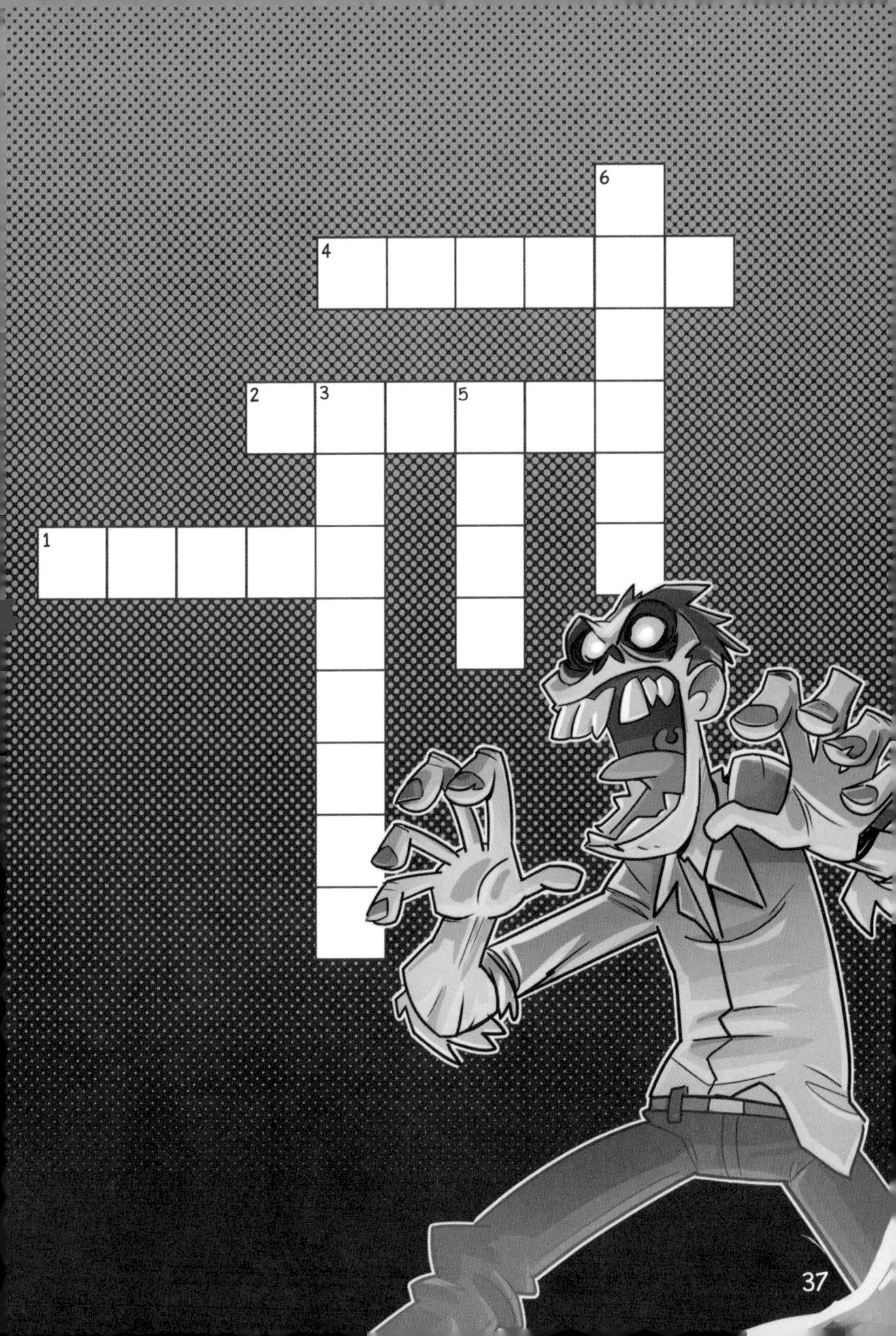
6
4
2
3
5
1

DUDDY'S FAVORITE CHARACTER WHEN HE WAS A KID WAS COLONEL CORN.

On the facing page, draw a hero who would be good at fighting zombies.

Create a name for your zombie hunter using words from the word bank.

BURNING

MASTER

INSANE

DOCTOR

PLAGUE

HEADSHOT

TERROR

HEAVY

FIRE

WARRIOR

FURY

EVIL

<Zombie hunter name>

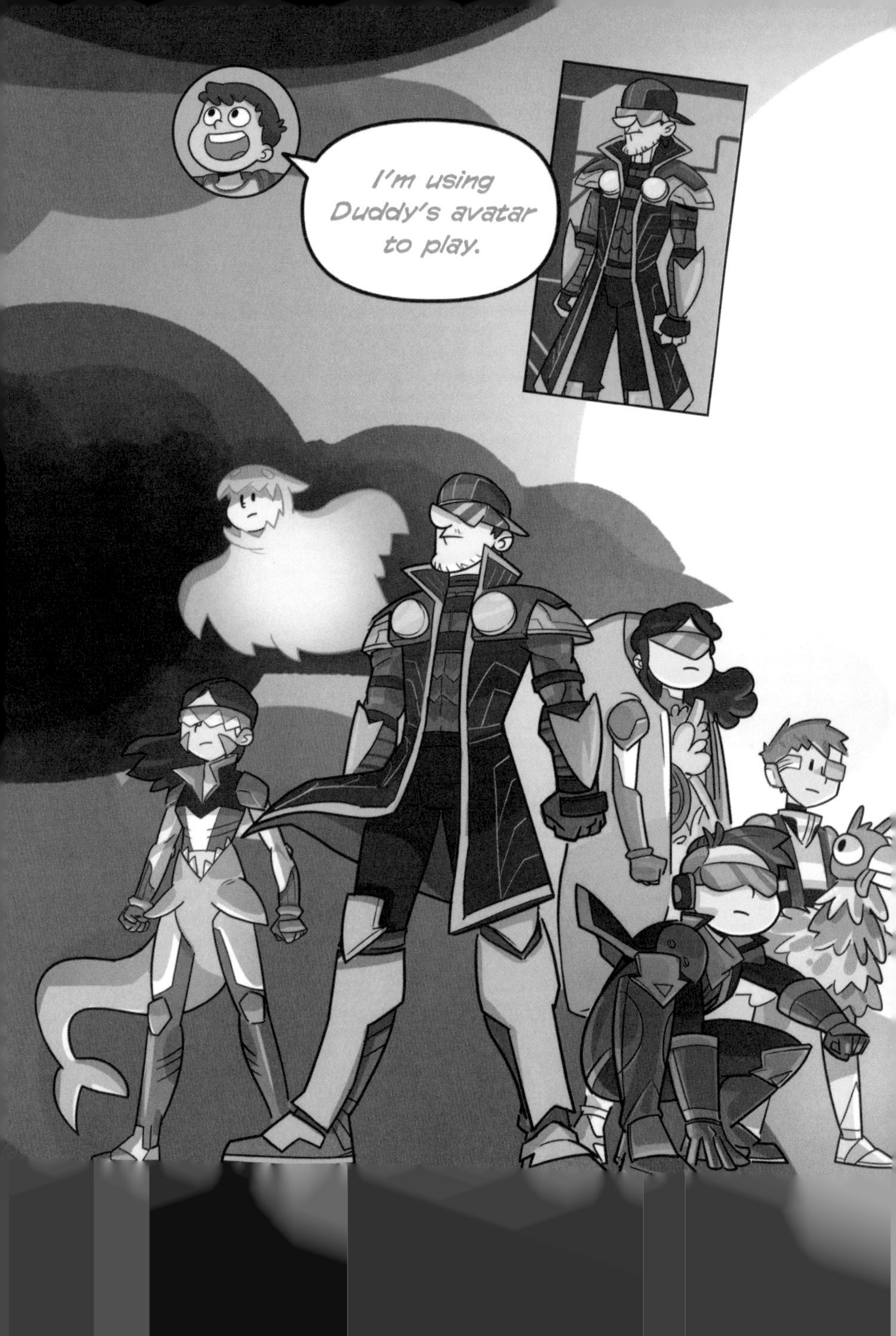
I'm using Duddy's avatar to play.

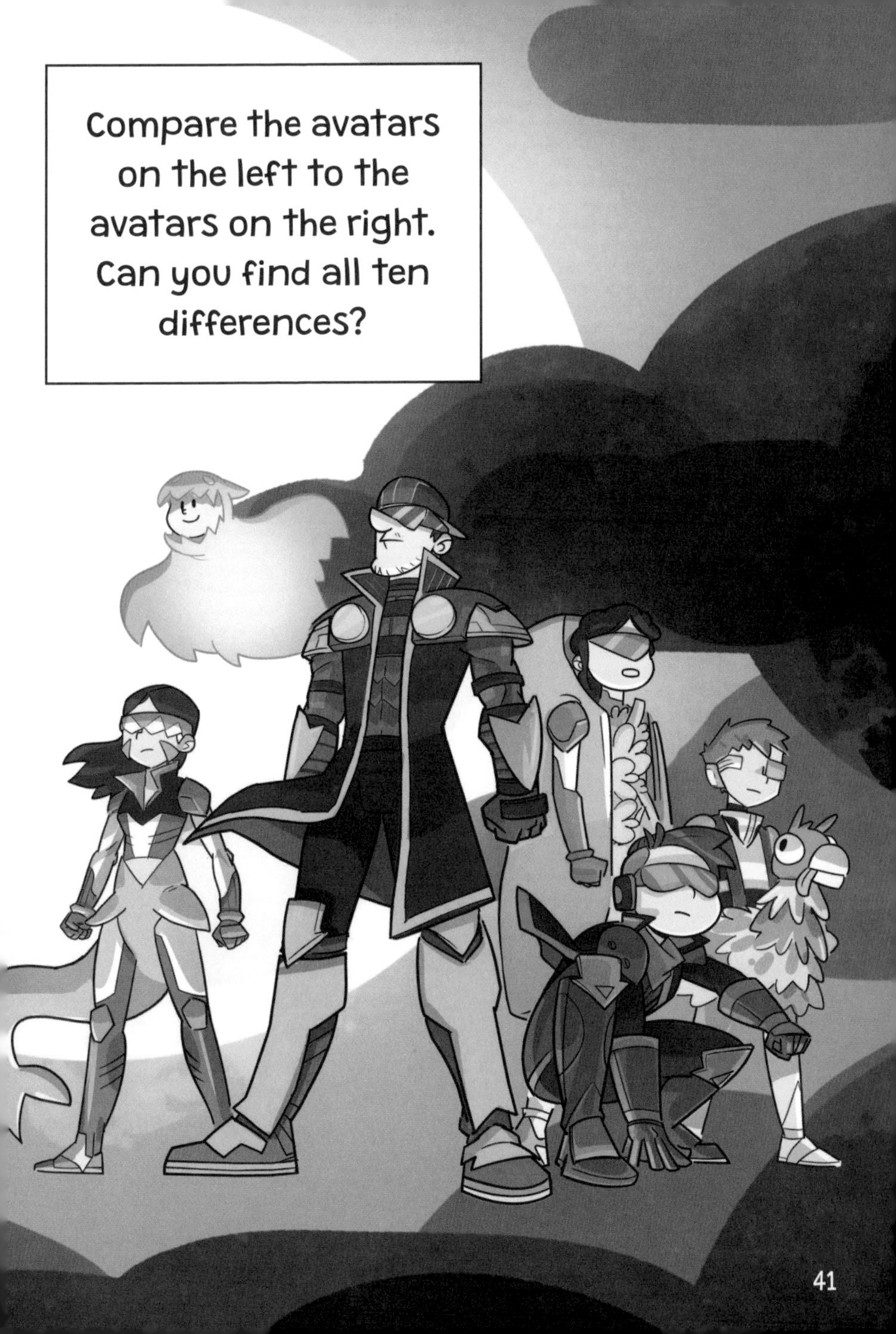
Compare the avatars on the left to the avatars on the right. Can you find all ten differences?

SHAWN'S AVATAR
IN THE GAME IS
A GHOST.

What's a ghost's favorite game?

Use the key below to find the answer.

1 = E   6 = A

2 = I   7 = K

3 = D   8 = N

4 = S   9 = R

5 = H

DANCE BREAK!

BEEN GAMING TOO LONG? JUMP UP AND BOOGIE DOWN FOR 15 SECONDS. SHOW OFF YOUR BEST MOVES!

IN *ZOMBIE BATTLES*, THE MILITIA MUST ESCAPE THE ZOMBIES.

Flip a coin to help them get away.

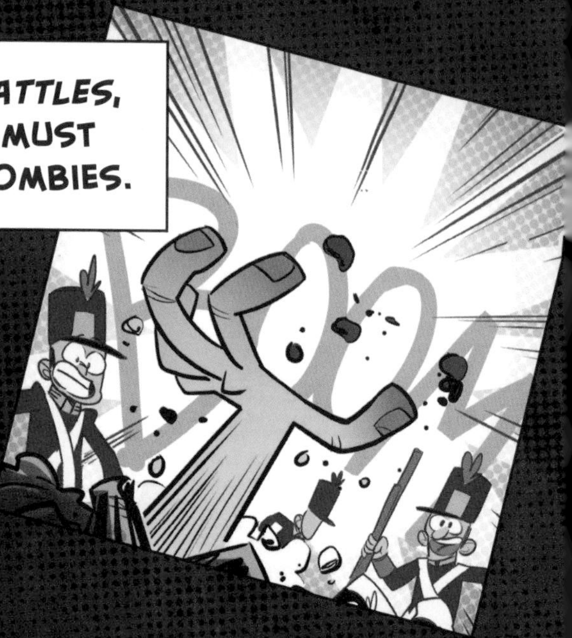

Start

Heads = move two spaces forward
Tails = move one space forward
Follow the instructions on the stair where you land.
If it's blank, flip the coin again.
Try to reach the finish line in as few coin flips as possible.

Move back one

Move forward two

Move back one

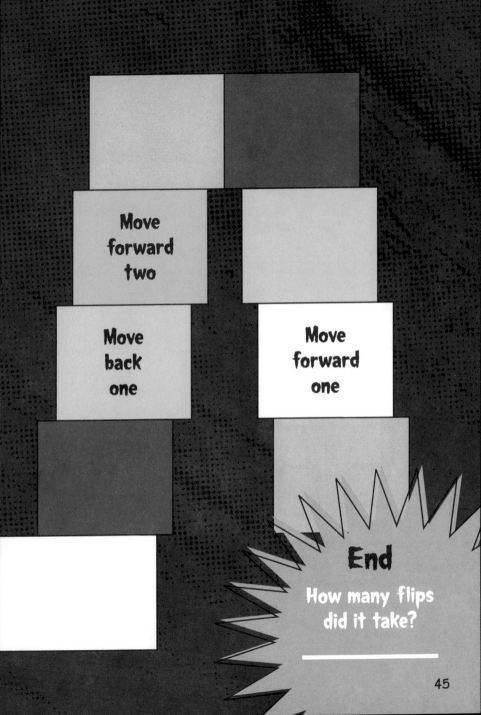

Move
forward
two

Move
back
one

Move
forward
one

End

How many flips
did it take?

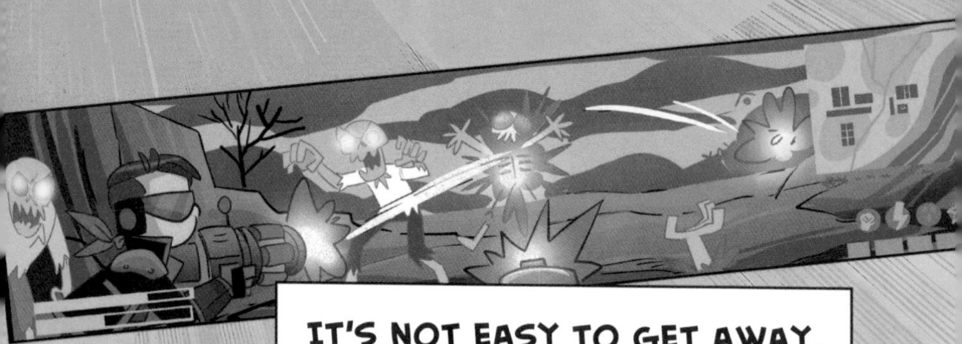

IT'S NOT EASY TO GET AWAY. MIKE HAS TO TRY A BUNCH OF DIFFERENT ROUTES.

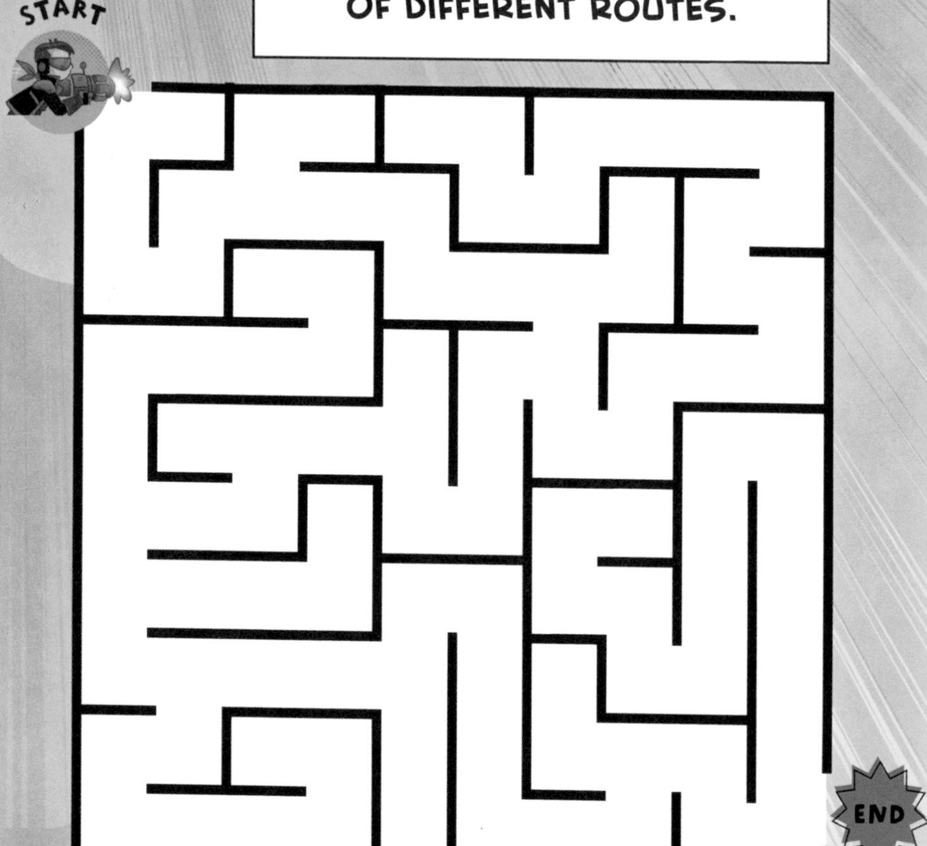
START
END

START

END

47

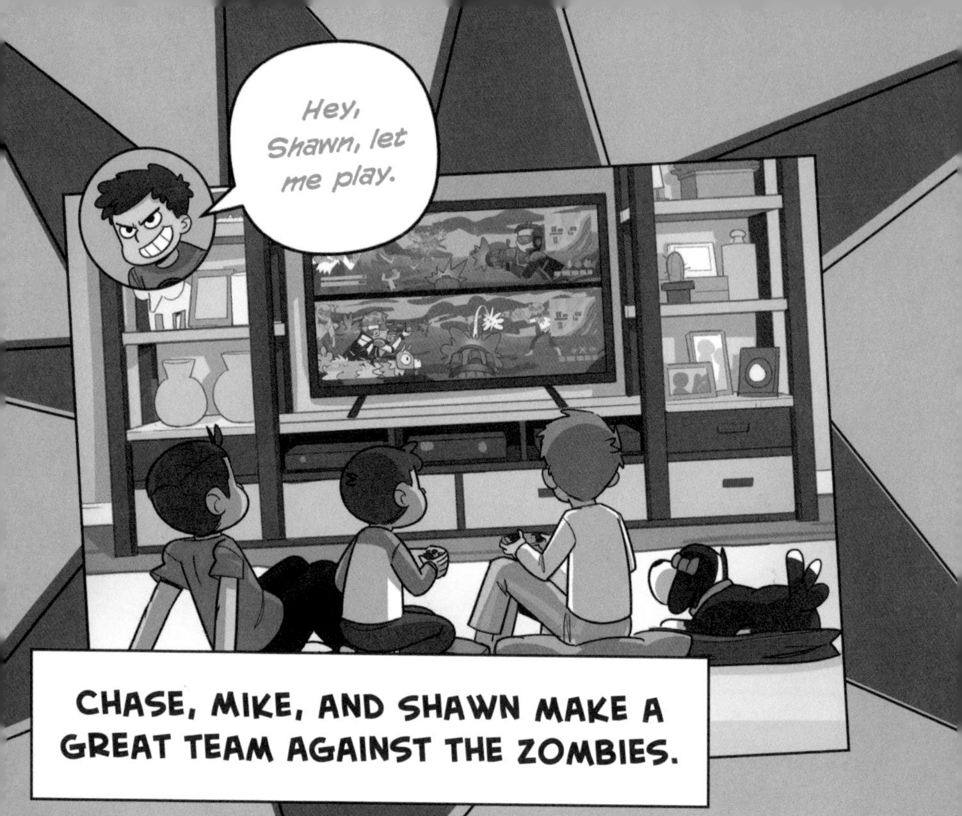
Hey, Shawn, let me play.
CHASE, MIKE, AND SHAWN MAKE A GREAT TEAM AGAINST THE ZOMBIES.

WHAT POWERS HELP THEM GET AWAY? FIND THE WORDS BELOW IN THE SEARCH ON THE NEXT PAGE.

run	shoot	escape
jump	clone	battle
hide	power up	kick
punch	hop	blast

```
O  Z  G  H  H  P  E  K  H  V  U
K  X  K  C  O  Y  L  R  C  C  C
K  V  N  H  F  A  T  N  C  I  J
W  U  S  H  O  O  T  U  A  U  K
P  I  I  S  B  M  A  R  M  A  K
Z  C  J  F  L  L  B  P  O  G  R
B  E  A  C  E  F  S  E  D  I  H
P  H  P  U  L  K  D  R  B  Q  Z
L  X  U  A  N  O  G  N  L  W  J
O  K  D  G  C  G  N  S  A  M  Q
W  P  B  N  S  S  X  E  S  X  B
F  E  W  Y  M  Z  E  X  T  Q  C
P  U  R  E  W  O  P  I  M  C  F
O  H  S  Y  F  C  F  V  L  C  L
S  K  I  O  Y  C  J  I  L  K  E
Z  O  H  L  S  Q  G  B  K  I  I
```

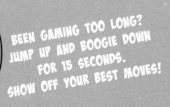

DANCE BREAK!

BEEN GAMING TOO LONG?
JUMP UP AND BOOGIE DOWN
FOR 15 SECONDS.
SHOW OFF YOUR BEST MOVES!

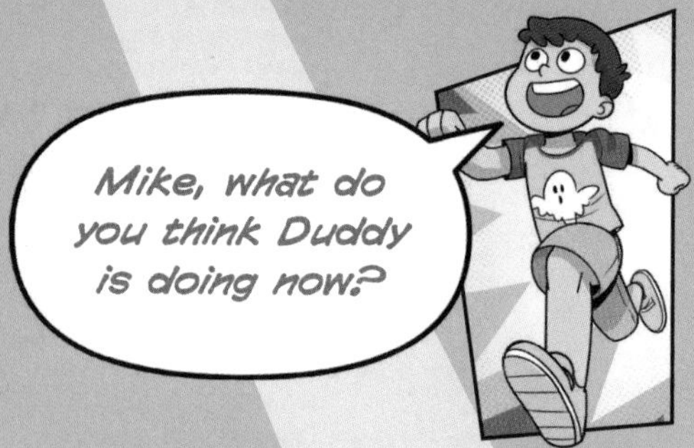
Mike, what do you think Duddy is doing now?

Swap the letters for some ideas.

1 = A	10 = J	19 = S
2 = B	11 = K	20 = T
3 = C	12 = L	21 = U
4 = D	13 = M	22 = V
5 = E	14 = N	23 = W
6 = F	15 = O	24 = X
7 = G	16 = P	25 = Y
8 = H	17 = Q	26 = Z
9 = I	18 = R	

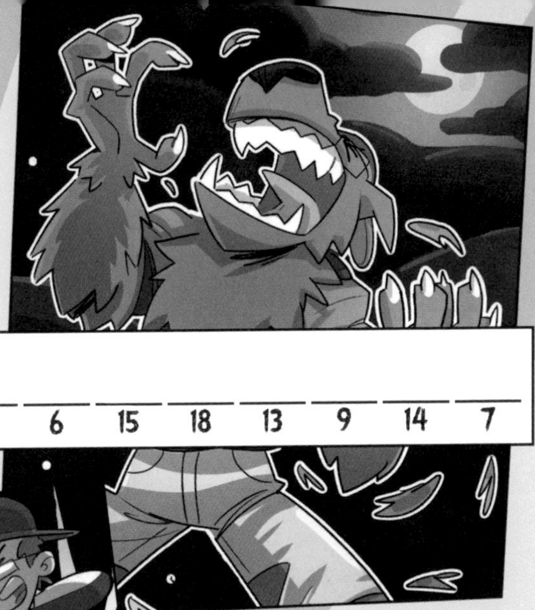

__ __ __ __ __ __ __ __ __ __ __ __
20 18 1 14 19 6 15 18 13 9 14 7

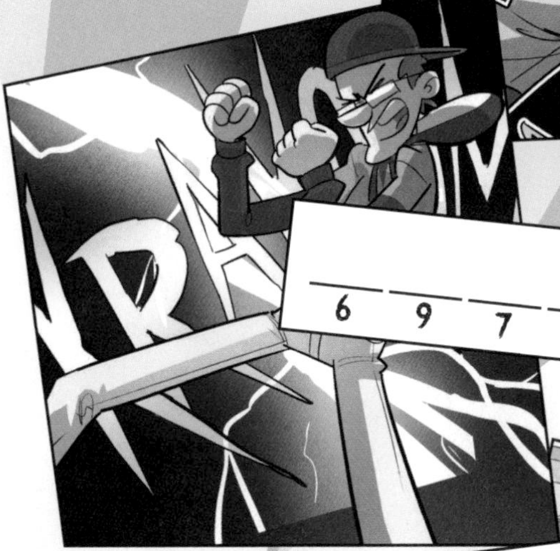

__ __ __ __ __ __ __ __
6 9 7 8 20 9 14 7

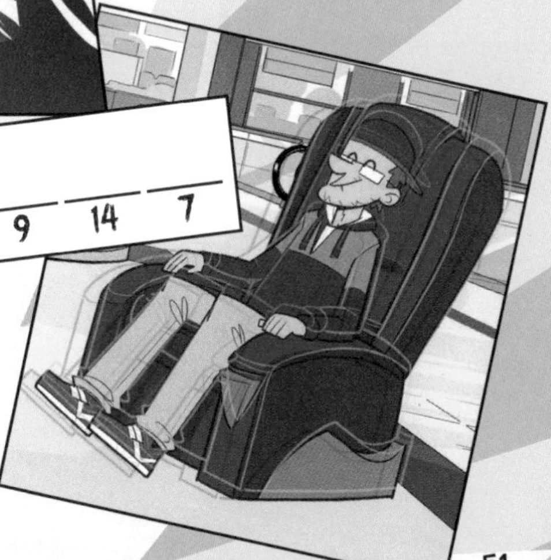

__ __ __ __ __ __ __ __
3 8 9 12 12 9 14 7

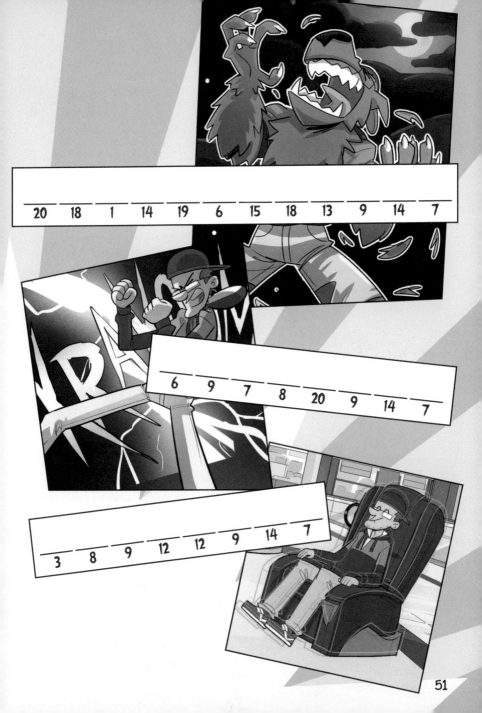

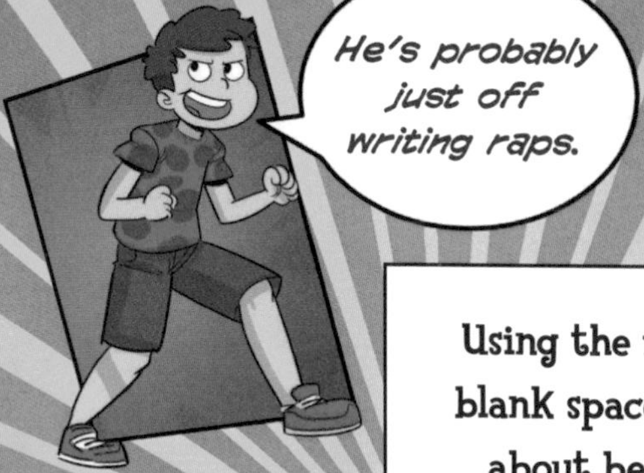
He's probably just off writing raps.

Using the words below, fill in the blank spaces to see Duddy's rhyme about being chased in a game.

find

crash

behind

fun

dash

run

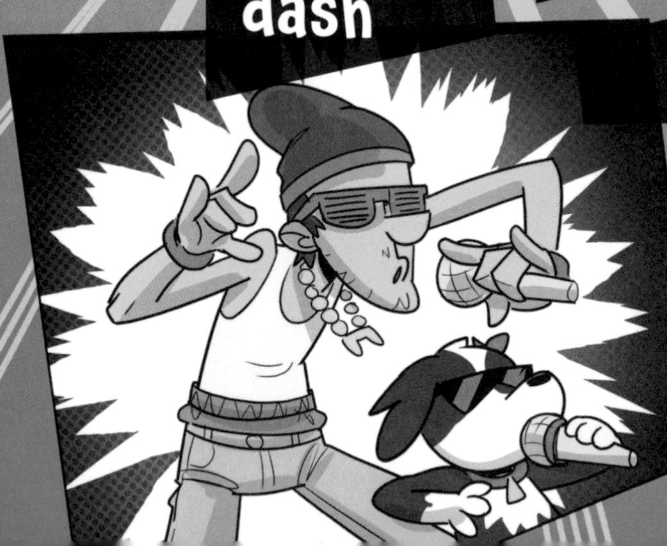

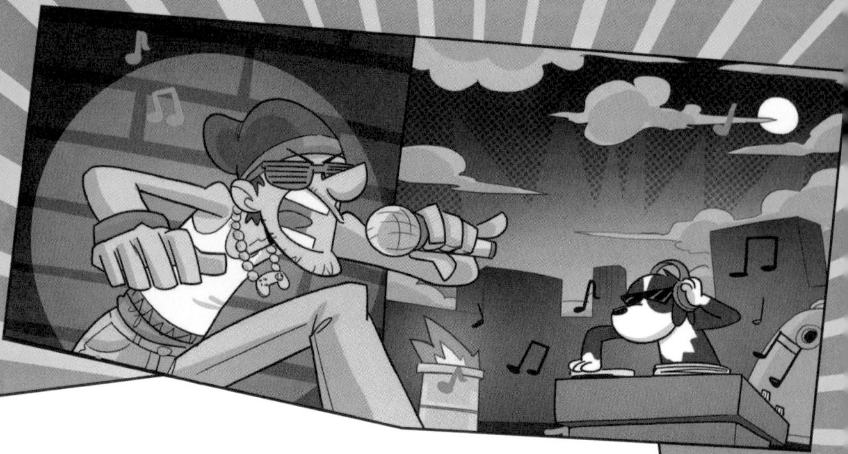

Oh my goodness,

He's right ________ me.

He's gonna ________ me.

I've gotta ________.

This ain't no ________.

Boom bash ________

I've gotta ________.

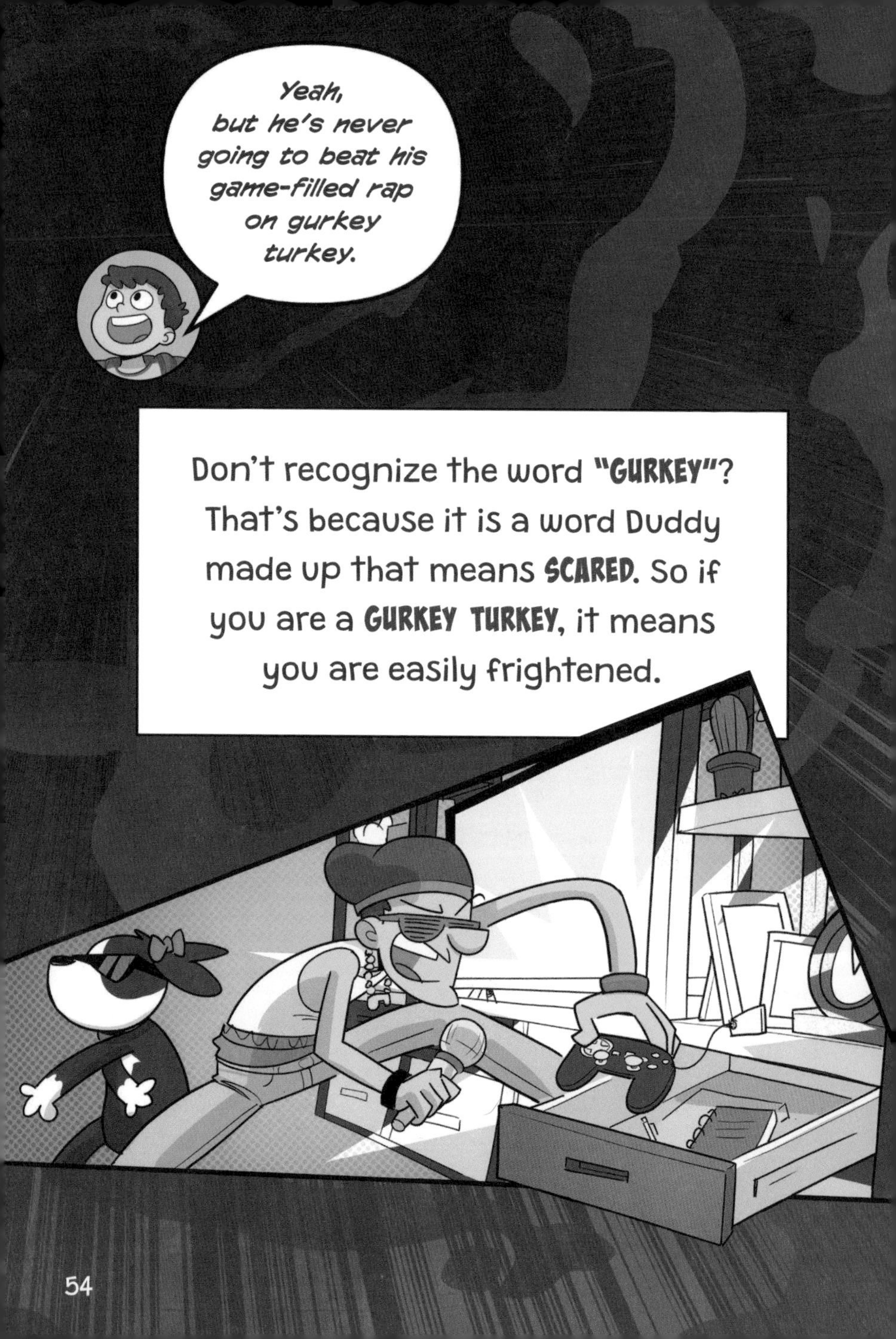
Yeah, but he's never going to beat his game-filled rap on gurkey turkey.
Don't recognize the word "GURKEY"? That's because it is a word Duddy made up that means SCARED. So if you are a GURKEY TURKEY, it means you are easily frightened.

Create ten words (or more!)
from the phrase
"I'M A GURKEY TURKEY"

_____

_____

_____

_____

_____

_____

_____

_____

_____

_____

EVEN THOUGH DUDDY'S RHYMES ARE TIGHT, HE'S NOT A GREAT SPELLER.

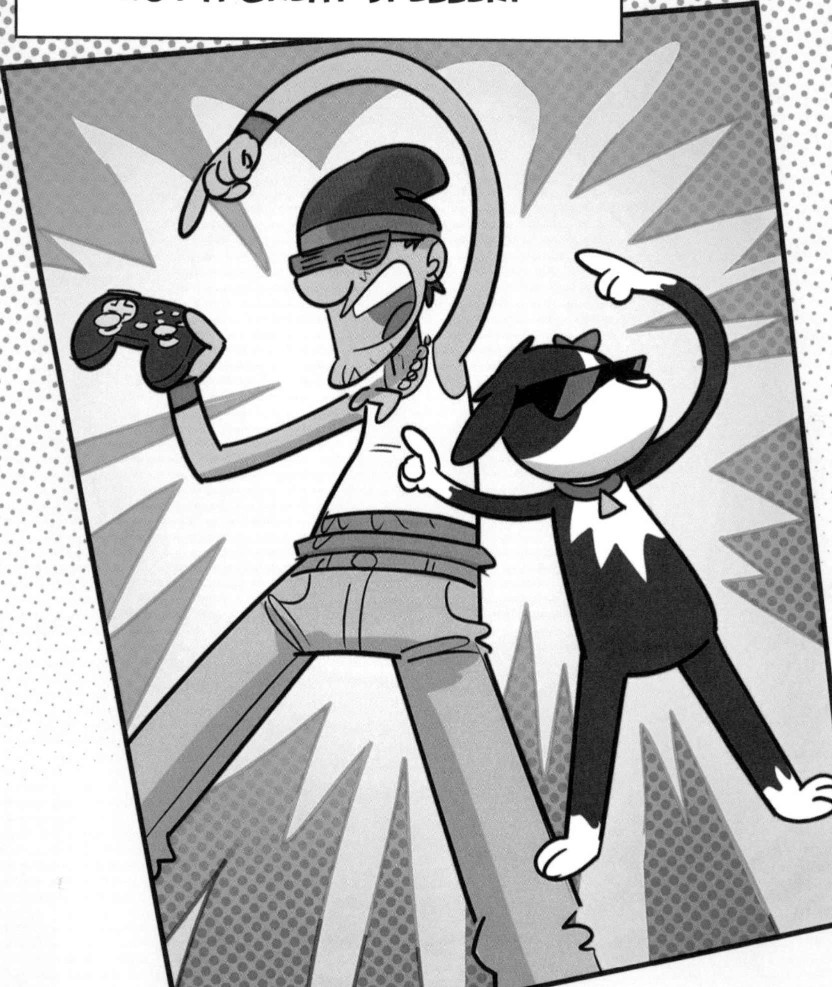

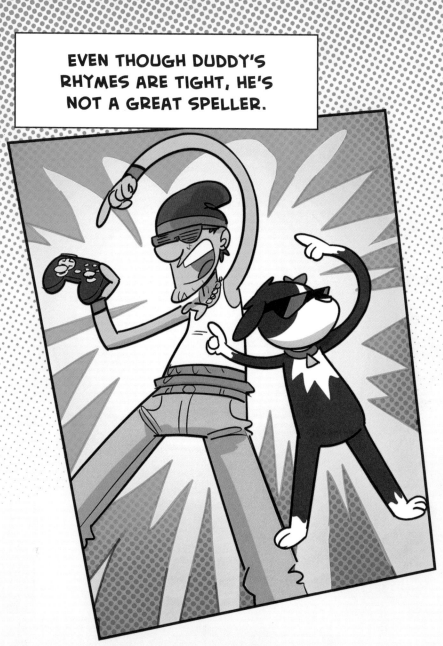

Circle the five misspelled words in the rap below:

Hey-yo, Pops, want to playe this game?

No thanks, kid, that looks lame.

No, I promese, it's really cool!

Yeah right, it looks old skool.

No! Try it, you mite like it!

All right, don't get so exsited.

DANCE BREAK!

BEEN GAMING TOO LONG? JUMP UP AND BOOGIE DOWN FOR 15 SECONDS. SHOW OFF YOUR BEST MOVES!

Duddy is probably at the game store, looking for classics.
BLOBBY FISH GAMES
APE CHASE!

Draw a scene from your favorite old-school video game.

Draw a line from Duddy through as many cheese balls as you can without running into Oreo.

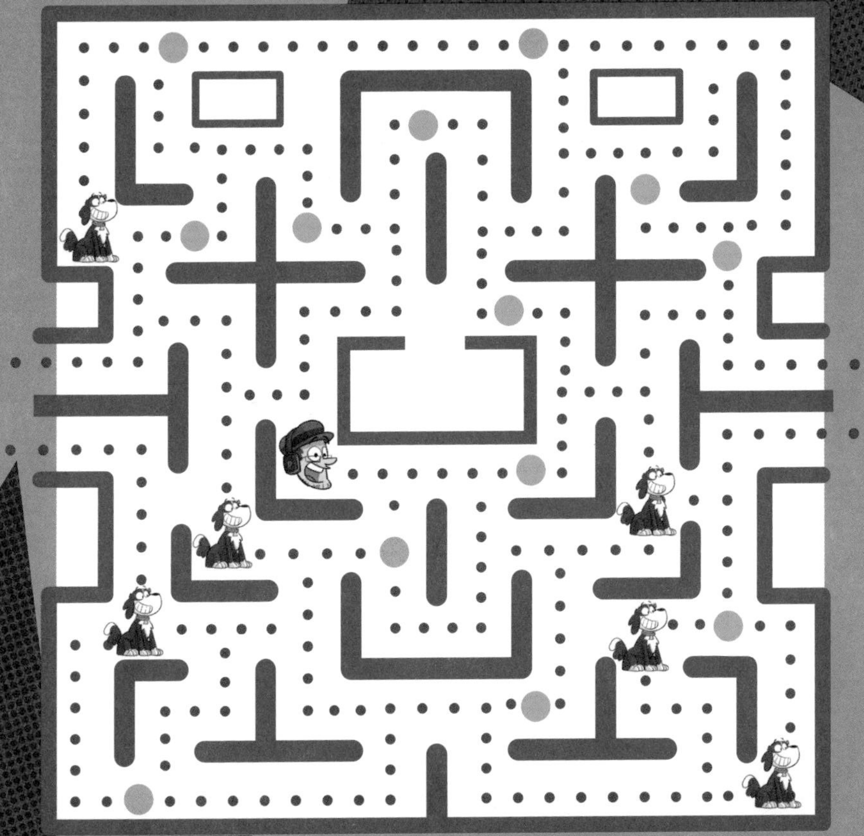

The most you can get is

______ .

If I was at the mall, I'd get a funnel cake.

WHAT WOULD YOU EAT?

Find and circle the FGTeeV fam favorites in the word search on the facing page.

- pizza
- ice cream
- french fries
- slushie

- gummy bears
- funnel cake
- hamburgers
- spaghetti

```
I  H  K  L  F  X  S  T  X  O  A  S
C  L  H  C  R  Q  L  L  D  C  Q  R
E  B  C  U  E  V  J  A  T  G  N  E
C  Q  T  R  N  C  H  W  M  P  G  G
R  E  K  A  C  L  E  N  N  U  F  R
E  P  V  I  H  Y  E  C  M  B  I  U
A  O  P  X  F  P  V  M  X  T  D  B
M  E  C  W  R  K  Y  D  T  X  C  M
T  Z  Y  S  I  B  C  E  Q  F  I  A
B  L  V  P  E  I  H  T  W  X  H  H
P  R  Y  A  S  G  J  Z  K  O  H  I
O  I  R  B  A  J  N  R  R  U  W  I
W  S  Z  P  S  L  U  S  H  I  E  X
P  D  S  Z  X  V  C  D  Q  R  L  M
R  O  A  I  A  Q  K  M  Y  T  J  B
```

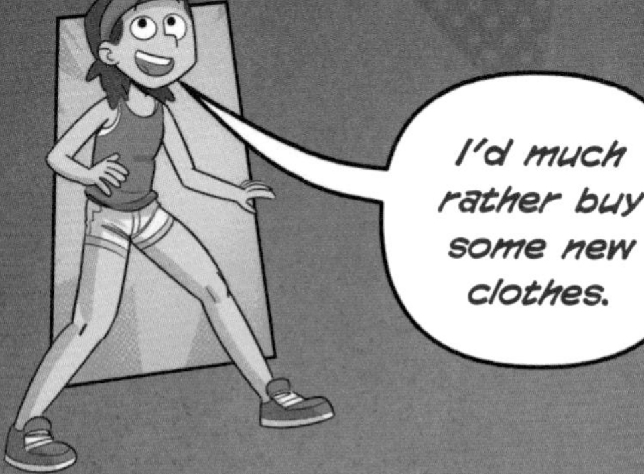
I'd much rather buy some new clothes.

Circle the pants Lexi would want.

Hint: the ones not covered in condiments!

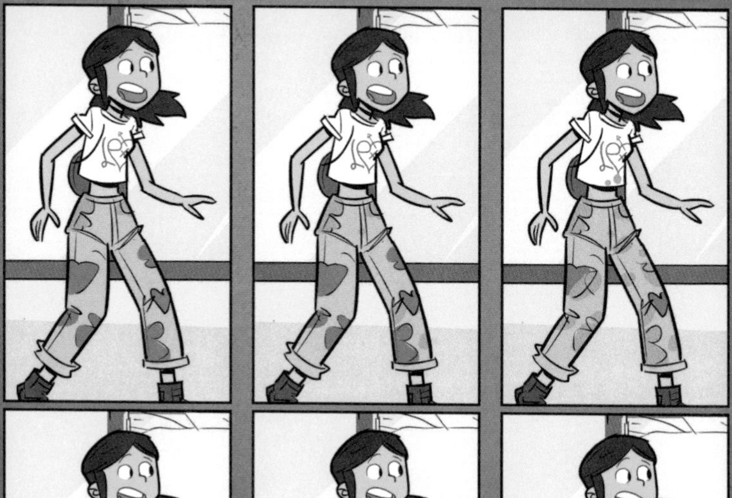

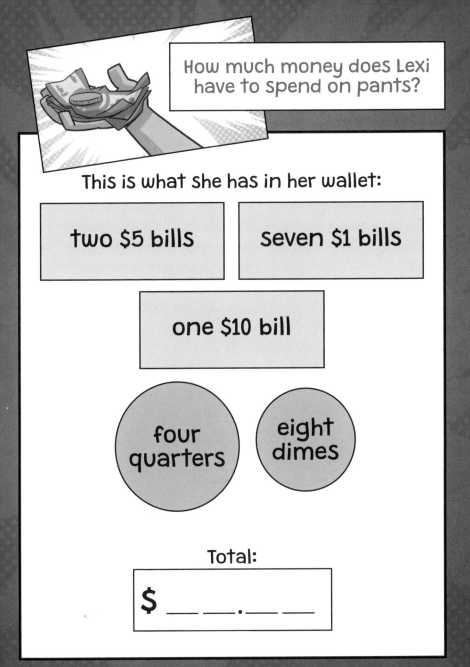

How much money does Lexi have to spend on pants?

This is what she has in her wallet:

two $5 bills

seven $1 bills

one $10 bill

four quarters

eight dimes

Total:

$ __ __ . __ __

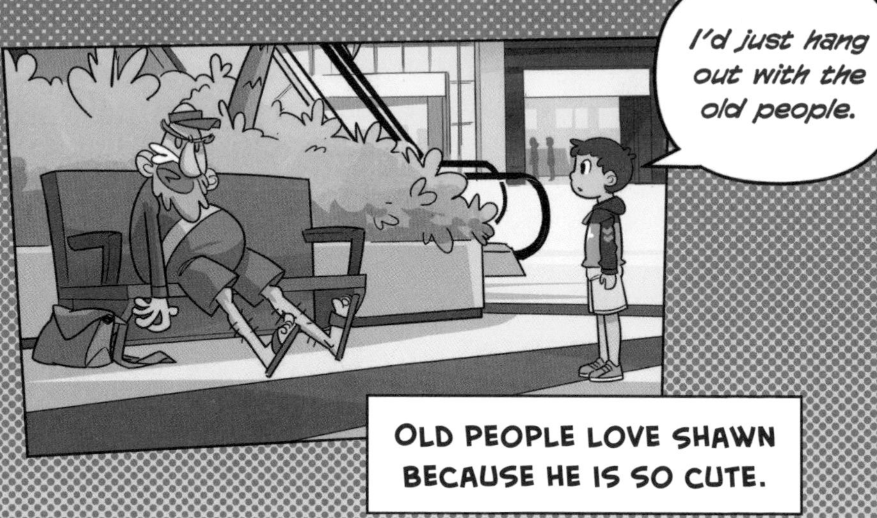
I'd just hang out with the old people.
OLD PEOPLE LOVE SHAWN BECAUSE HE IS SO CUTE.

Circle words old people might use to describe Shawn.

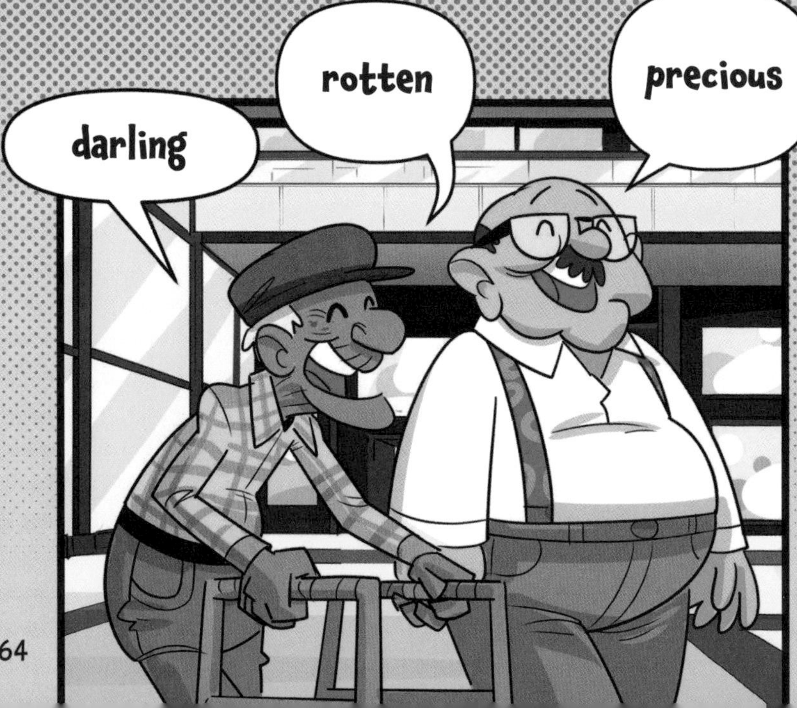
darling
rotten
precious

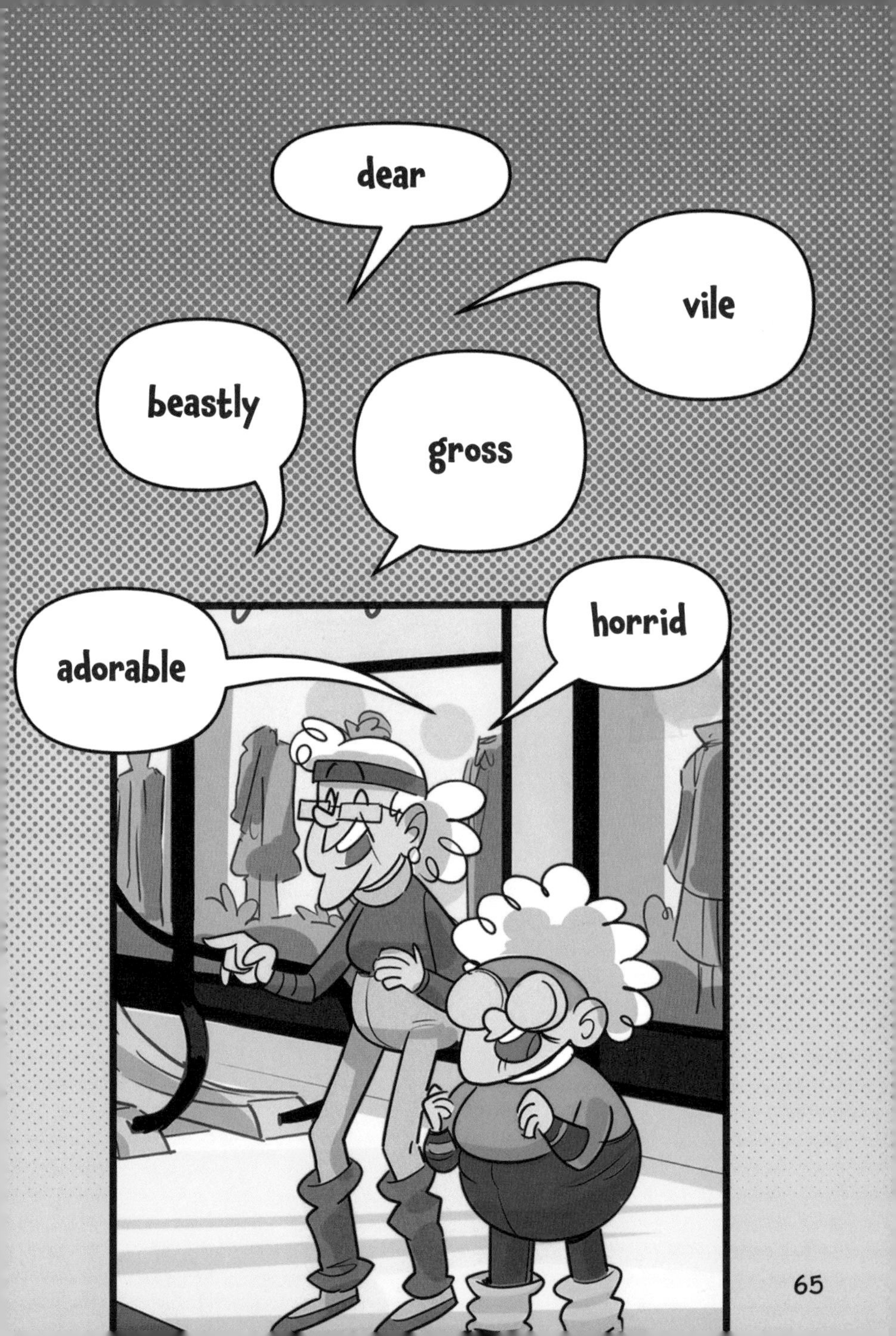
dear
vile
beastly
gross
adorable
horrid

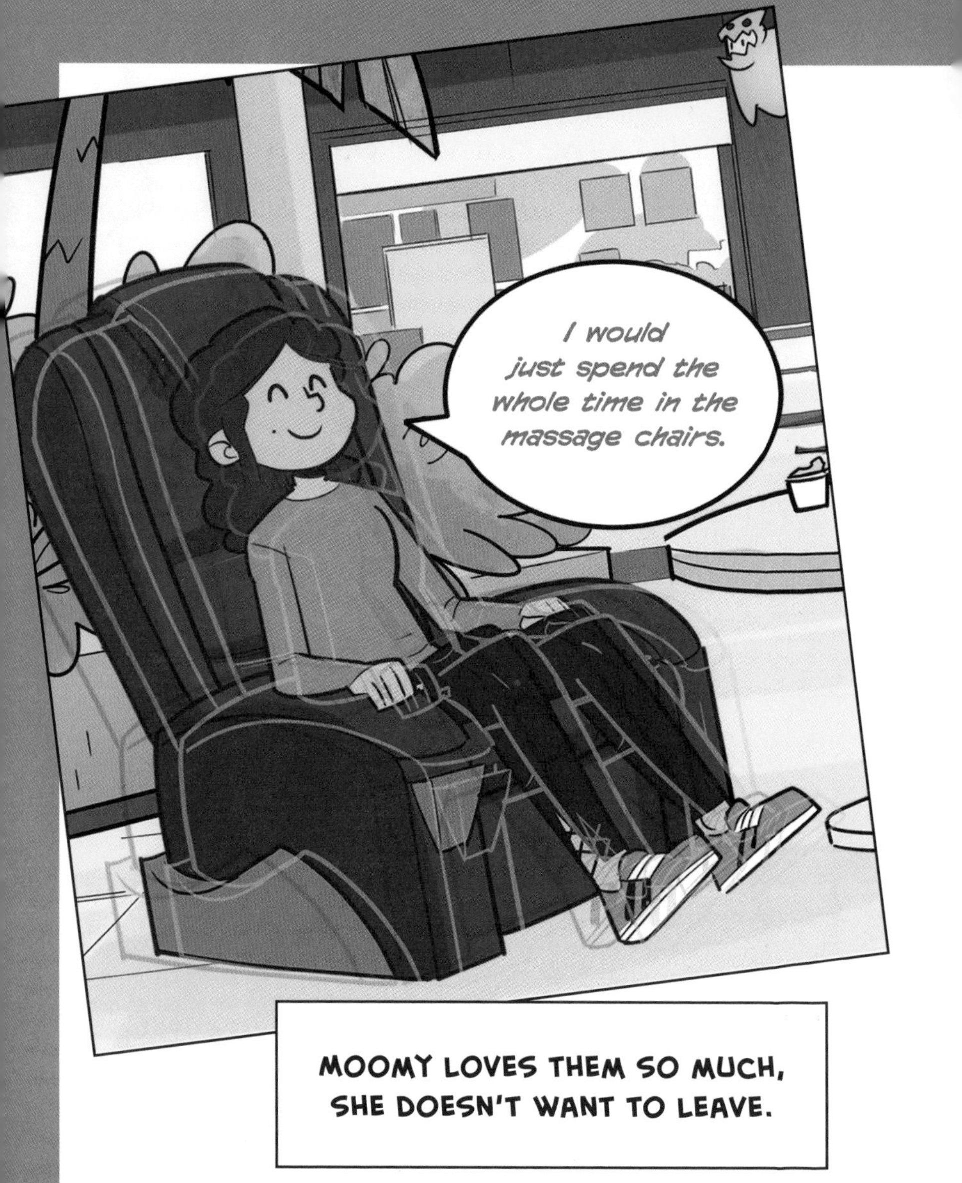
I would just spend the whole time in the massage chairs.

MOOMY LOVES THEM SO MUCH, SHE DOESN'T WANT TO LEAVE.

Complete the number patterns to get Moomy out of the mall:

5, ___, 21, 29, ___, 45

1, 3, 9, 27, ___

22, 29, ___, 43, ___

16, 13, ___, 7, ___

___, 4, 8, 16, ___

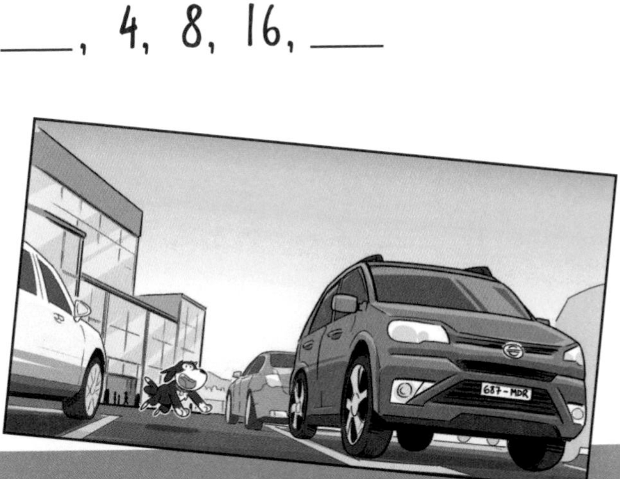
687-MDR

Knowing Duddz, he probably got lost in the mall.

Help Duddy get out of the mall by filling in the empty squares with one of the missing numbers (1–6) or the missing icons (■, ●, ★).

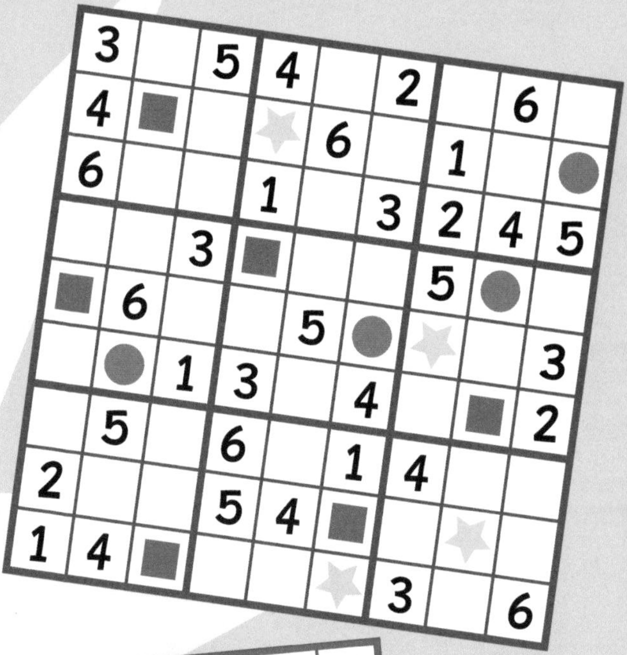

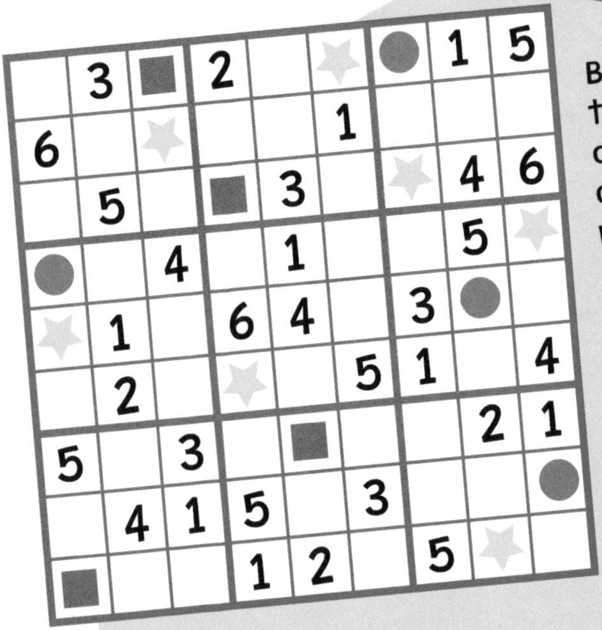

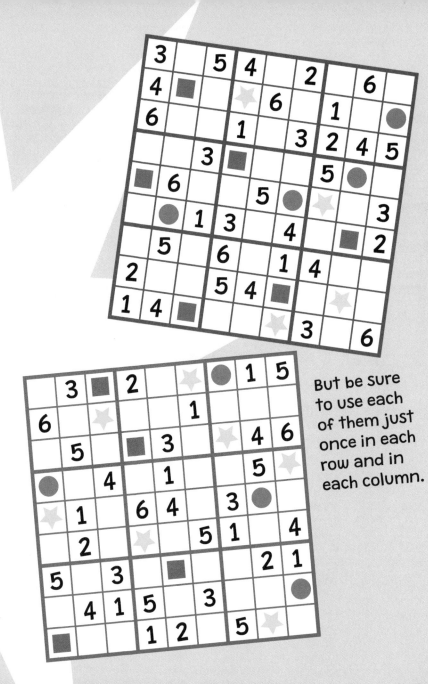

But be sure
to use each
of them just
once in each
row and in
each column.

Maybe he ran into Cecil at the game store?
Cecil is probably asking to come over to game.

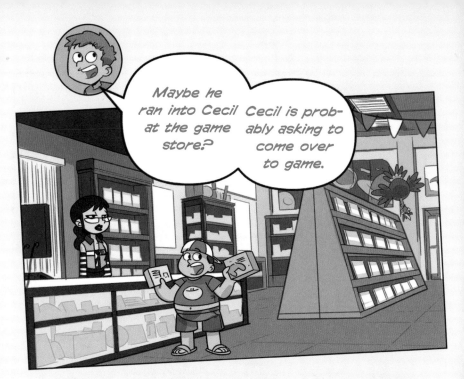

Cecil is the worst to game with because he freaks out if he loses. Use the numbers below to figure out Duddy's excuse for not having him over.

E = 5
M = 9
A = 7
G = 3
T = 11

I = 13
F = 1
S = 15
L = 17
Y = 19

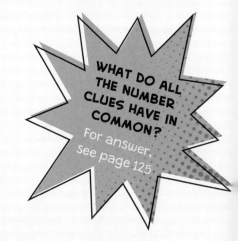

WHAT DO ALL THE NUMBER CLUES HAVE IN COMMON?

For answer, see page 125

___ 3 ___ 7 ___ 9 ___ 5

___ 11 ___ 13 ___ 9 ___ 5 ___ 13 ___ 15

___ 1 ___ 7 ___ 9 ___ 13 ___ 17 ___ 19

___ 11 ___ 13 ___ 9 ___ 5

DANCE BREAK!

BEEN GAMING TOO LONG? JUMP UP AND BOOGIE DOWN FOR 15 SECONDS. SHOW OFF YOUR BEST MOVES!

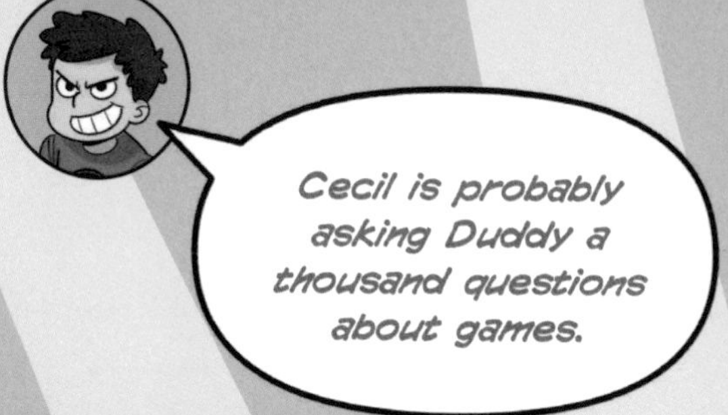
Cecil is probably asking Duddy a thousand questions about games.

Draw different expressions on Duddy's face as he struggles to answer Cecil's questions.

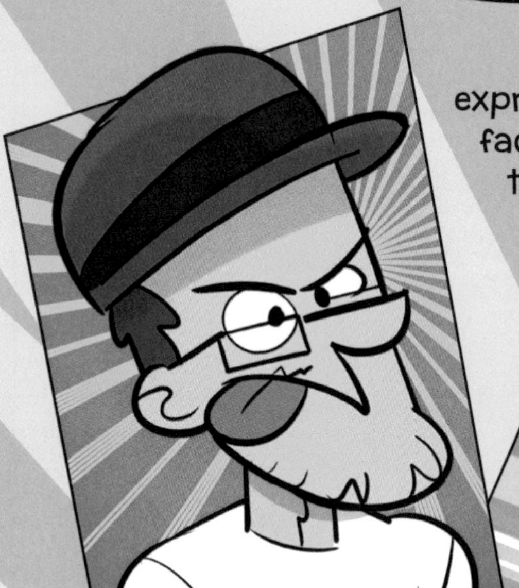

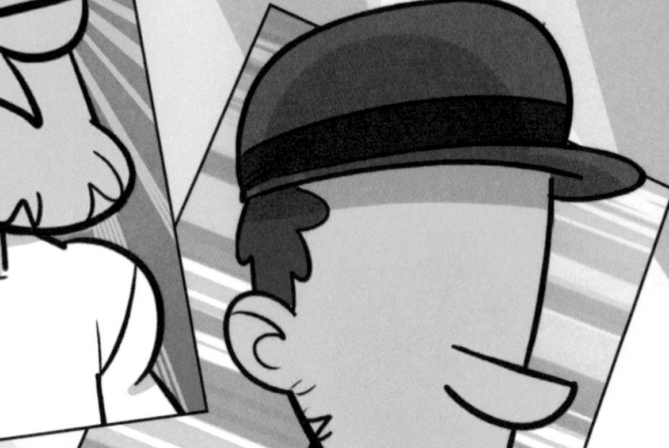

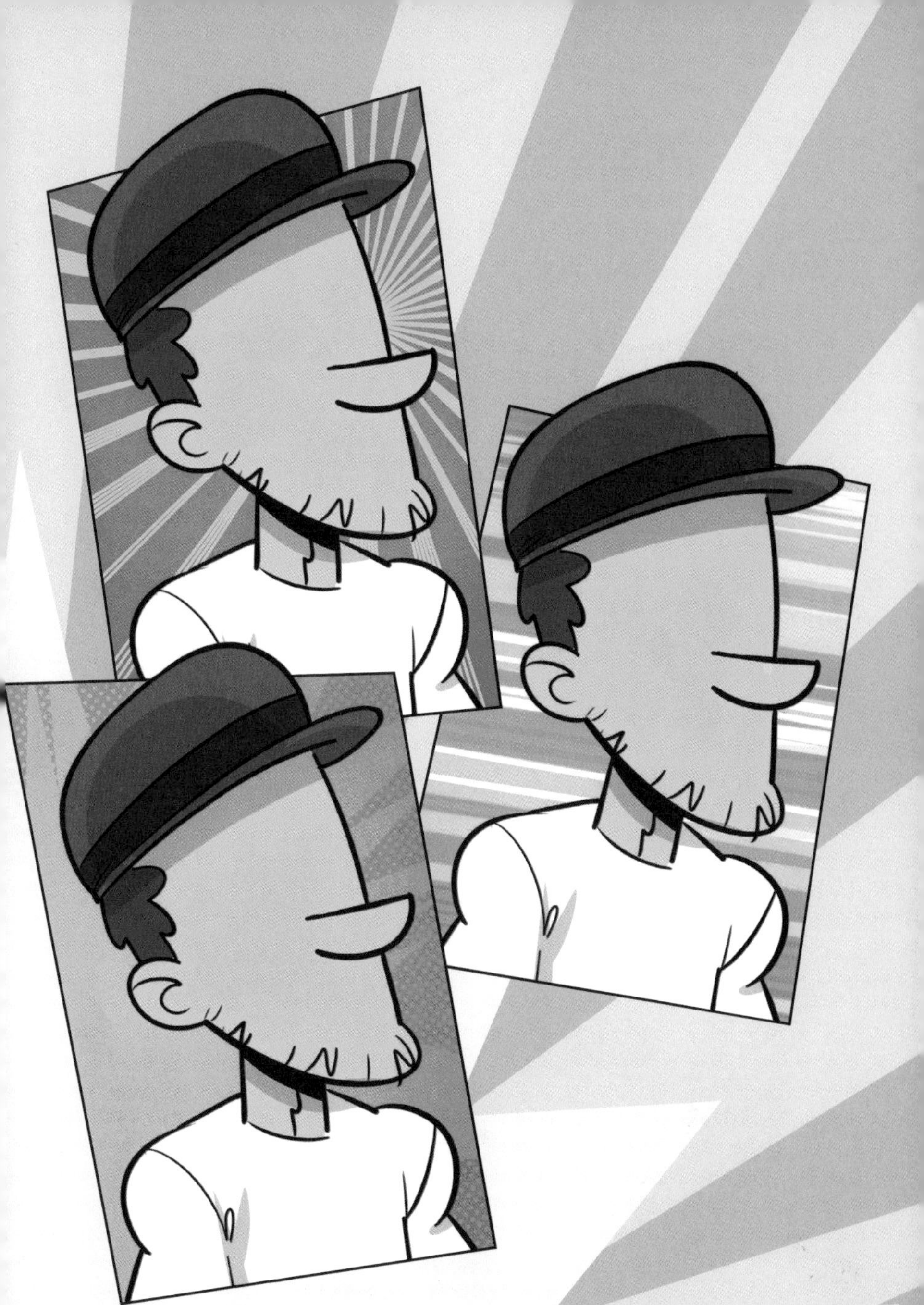

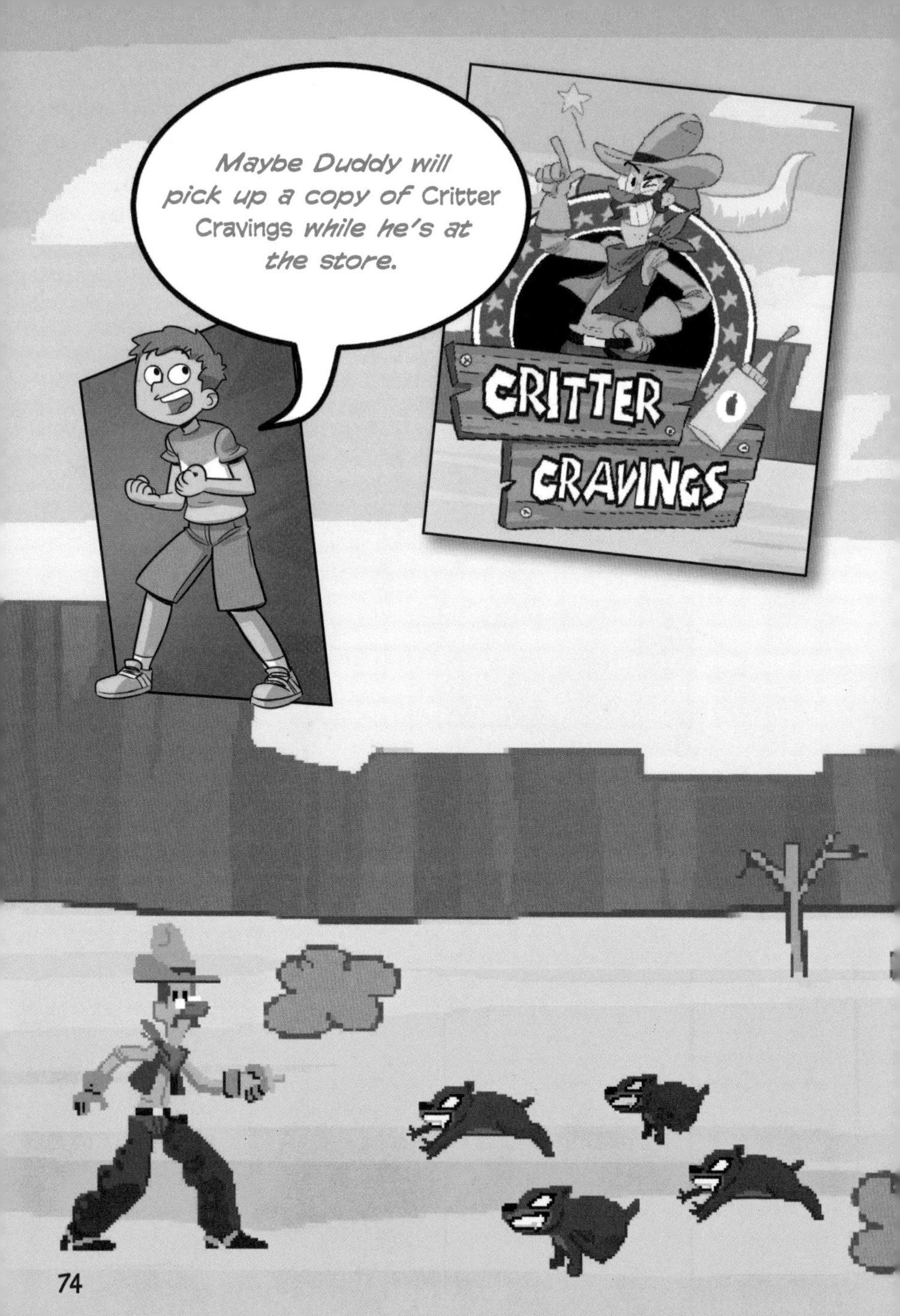
Maybe Duddy will pick up a copy of Critter Cravings while he's at the store.
CRITTER CRAVINGS

Create a list of ten critters, the first starting with the letter C. On the second line, write the name of a critter that begins with the second letter of your first word. And on the third line, write the name of a critter that begins with the second letter of your second word, and so on until you've filled in all ten.

C_____

_____

_____

_____

_____

_____

_____

_____

_____

_____

THE GOAL OF *CRITTER CRAVINGS* IS TO SAVE FRANKLIN'S LAND FROM INVADING ANIMALS.

Flip a coin to get relish weapons you'll need to fight them off.

Heads = move two spaces forward
Tails = move one space forward

Follow the instructions on the spot where you land.

If it's blank, flip the coin again.

Try to reach the finish line in as few coin flips as possible.

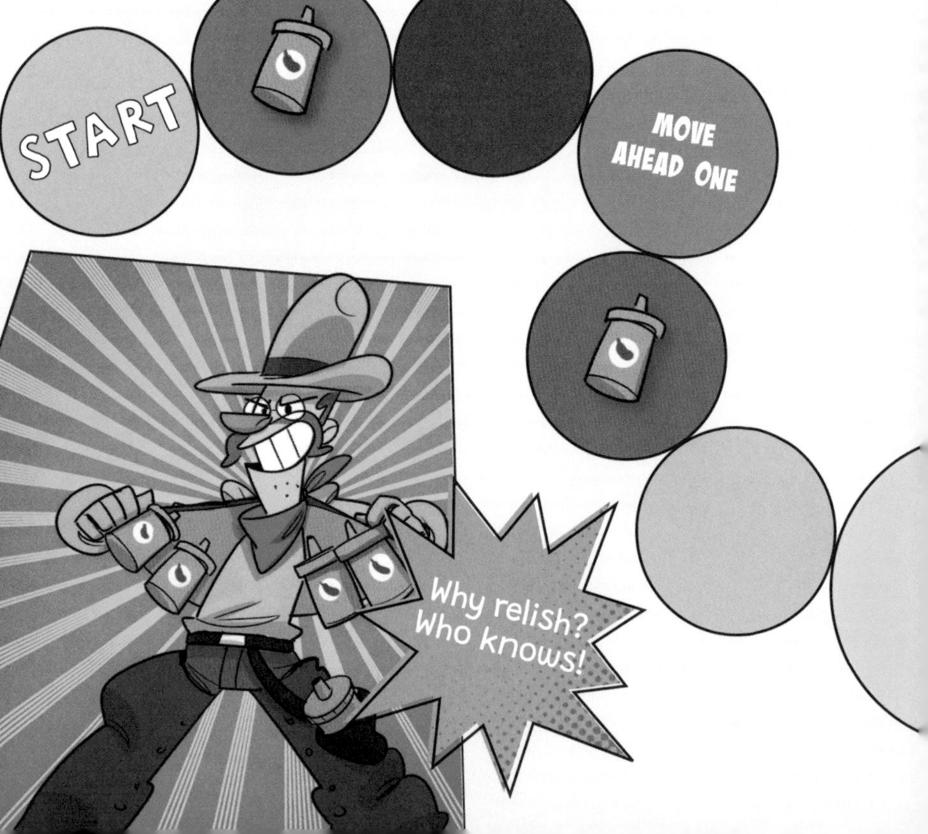
START
MOVE AHEAD ONE
Why relish? Who knows!

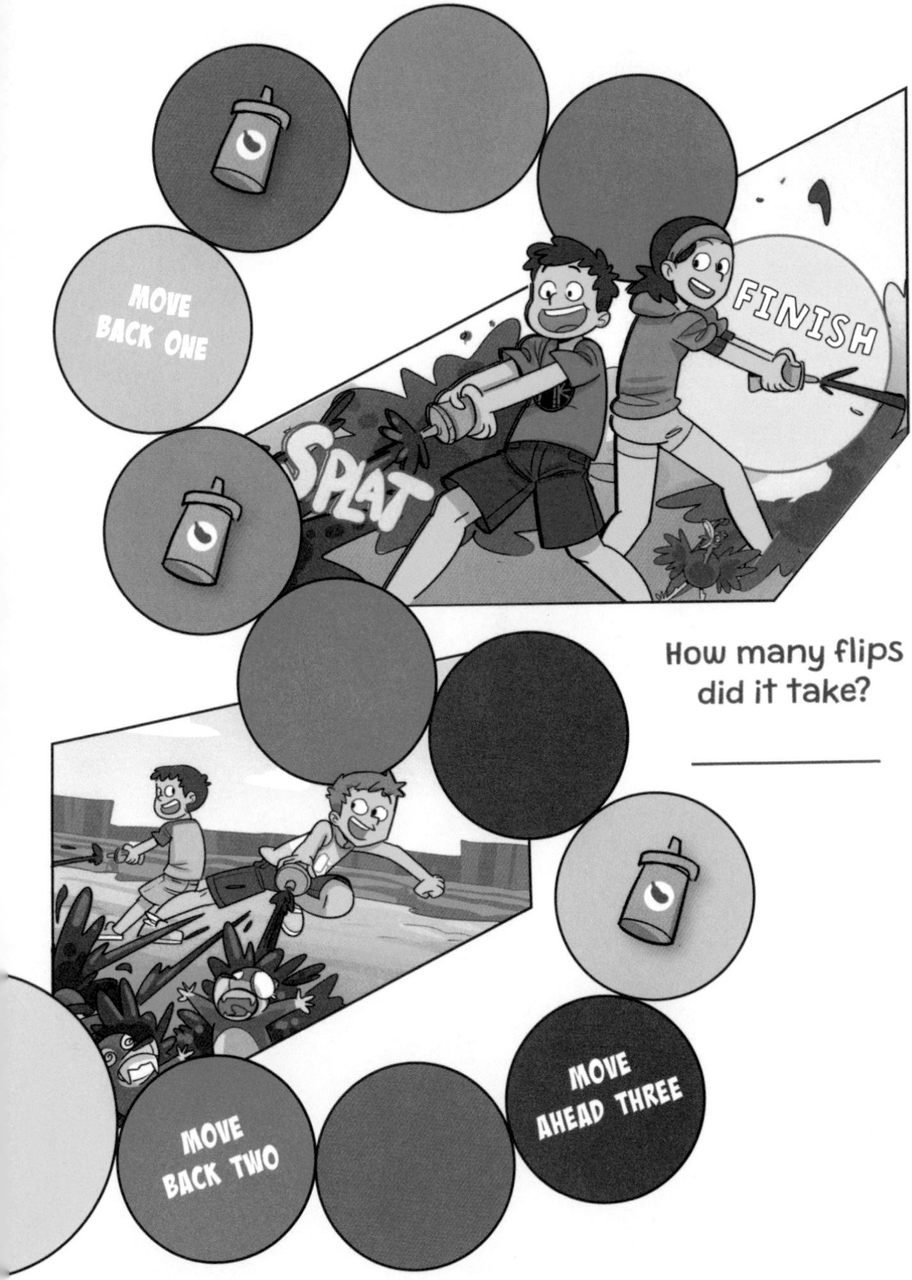
FINISH
MOVE BACK ONE
SPLAT
MOVE BACK TWO
MOVE AHEAD THREE

How many flips did it take?

____

IN THE FIRST LEVEL OF *CRITTER CRAVINGS*, PLAYERS FIGHT OFF KILLER PRAIRIE DOGS.

Find and circle the one prairie dog that seems friendly.

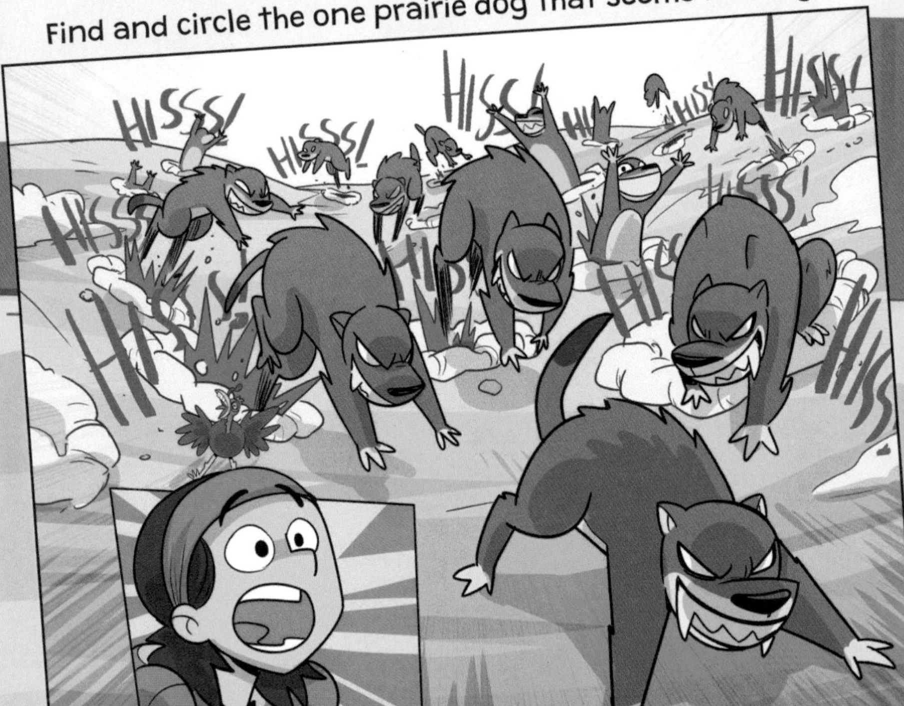
HISSS!
HISSS!
HISSS!

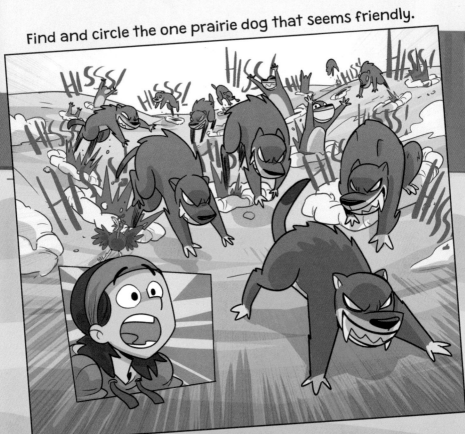

Prairie dogs live together in colonies in burrows underground. Draw an underground home for killer prairie dogs.

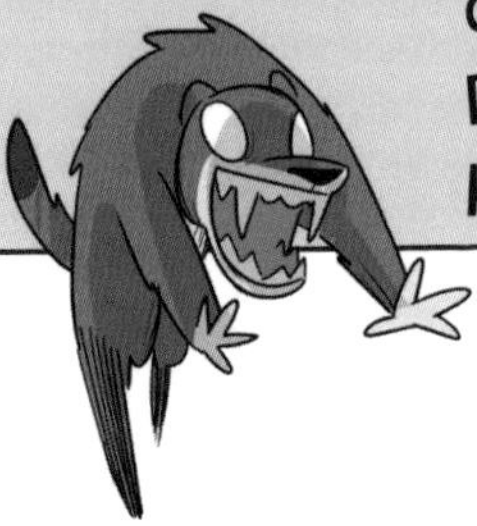

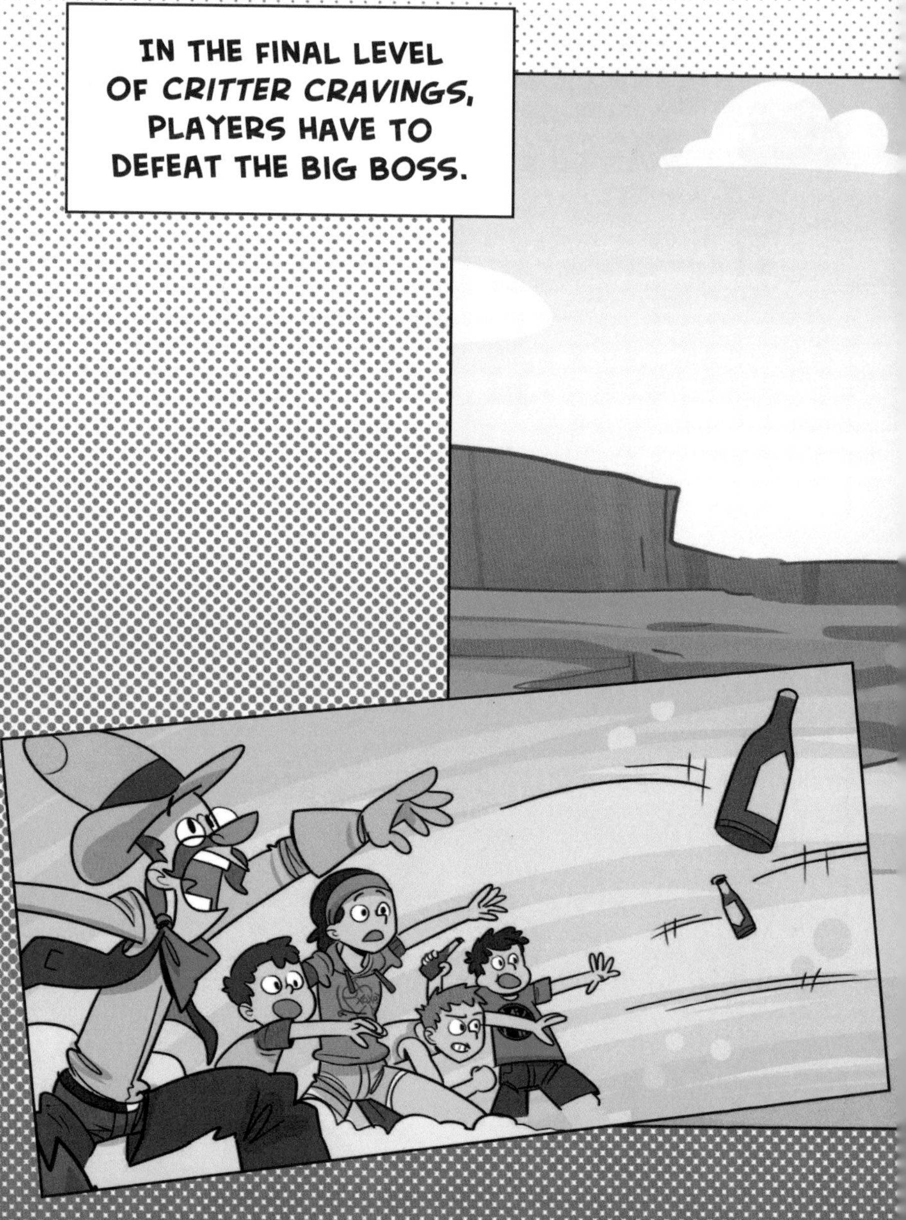
IN THE FINAL LEVEL OF *CRITTER CRAVINGS*, PLAYERS HAVE TO DEFEAT THE BIG BOSS.

Connect the dots to reveal the creature.

81

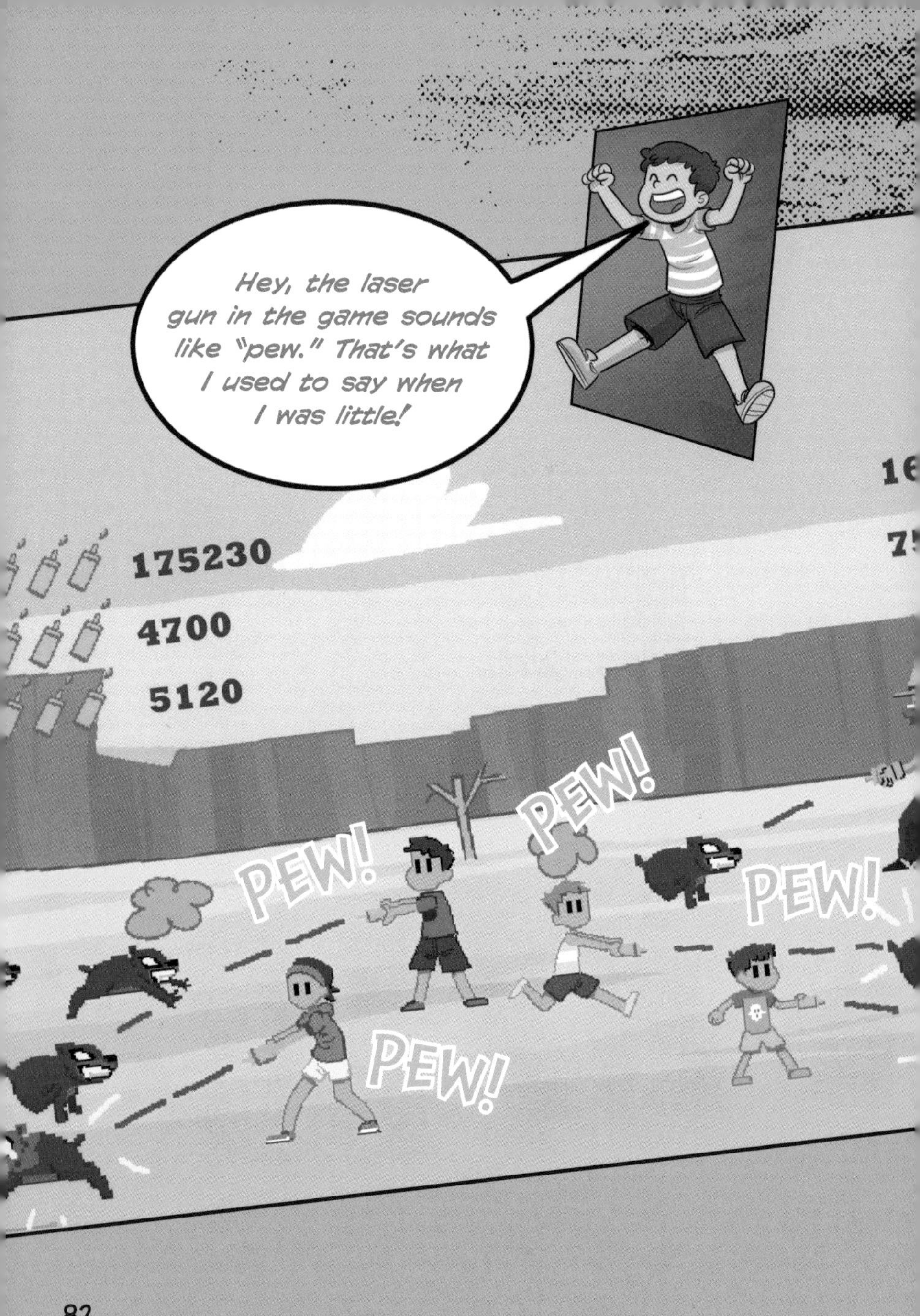
Hey, the laser gun in the game sounds like "pew." That's what I used to say when I was little!
175230
4700
5120
PEW!
PEW!
PEW!
PEW!

Unscramble the letters below to reveal other weapon sounds!

ambl   _____

gbna   _____

owp   _____

ahwm   _____

oo-abkm   _____

rccak   _____

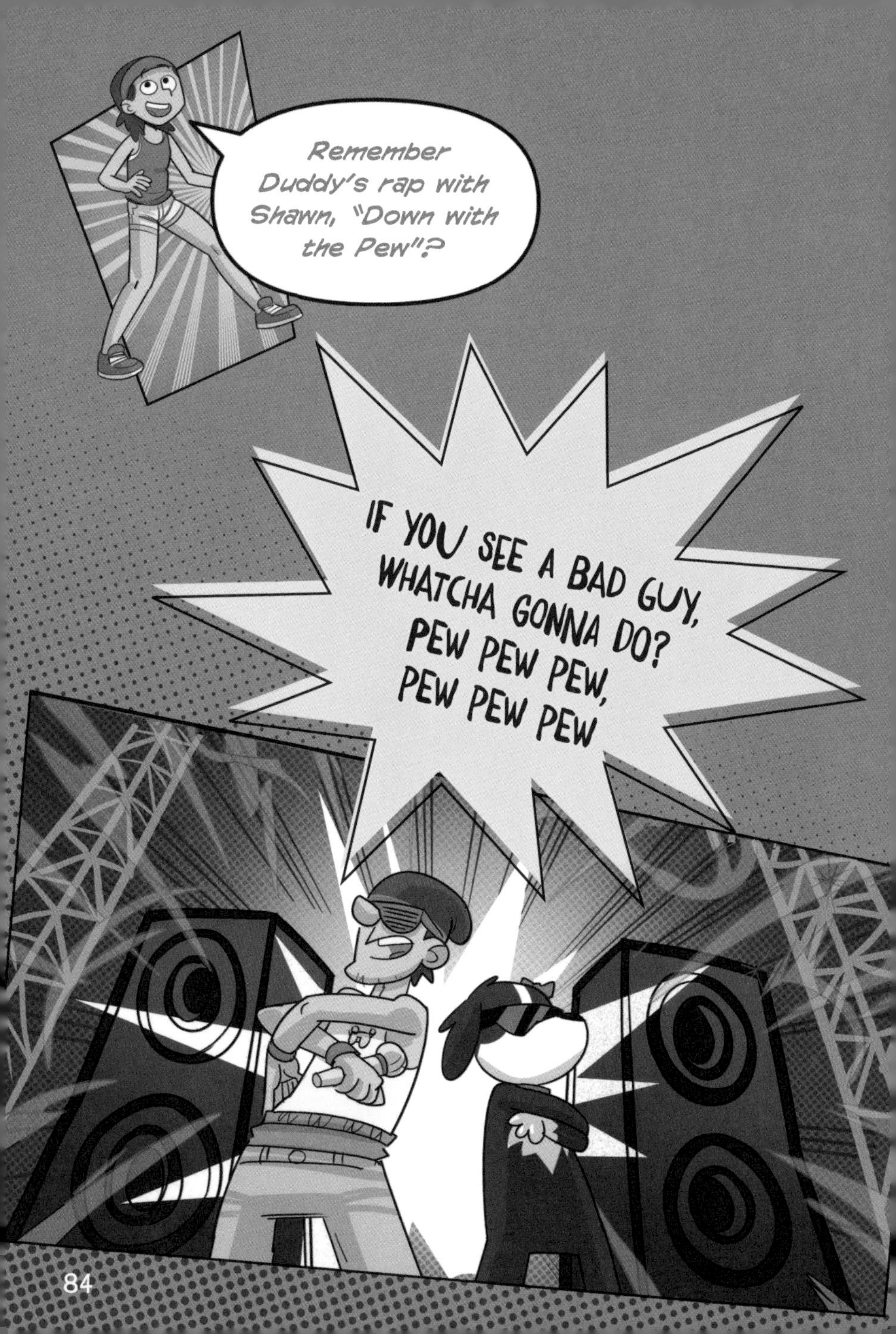
Remember Duddy's rap with Shawn, "Down with the Pew"?
IF YOU SEE A BAD GUY, WHATCHA GONNA DO? PEW PEW PEW, PEW PEW PEW

Fill in the rhyming words below to create your own verse of the song.

Get back, you ________

I'll be that ________

I'll aim to stop ________

All up in your side,
my bullets they ________

I be down with the ________

Tell me, is you down ________?

COPPER
PEW
YOU

ROBBER
TOO
GOT YOU

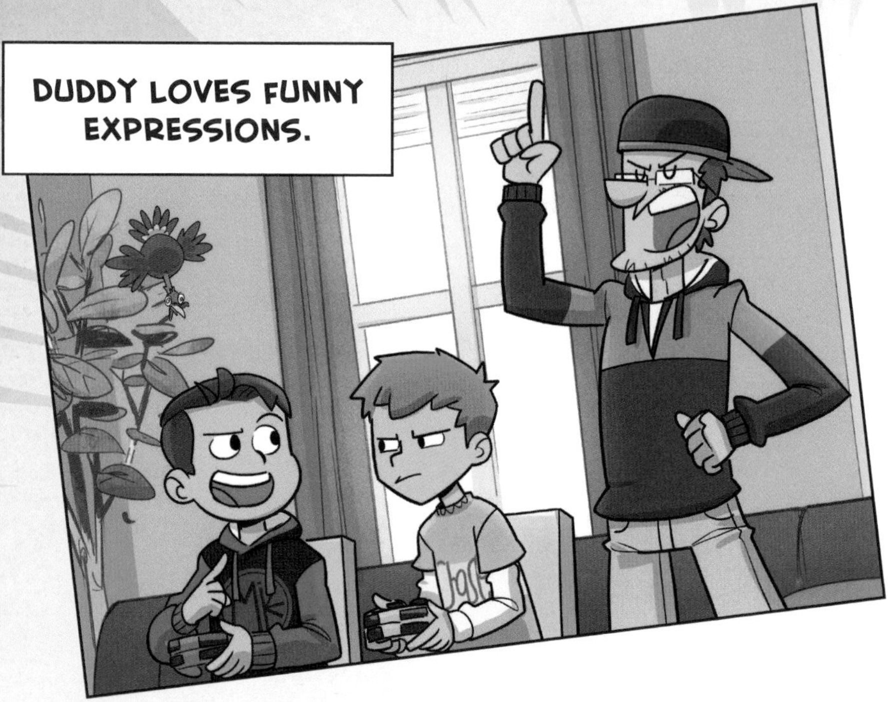
DUDDY LOVES FUNNY EXPRESSIONS.

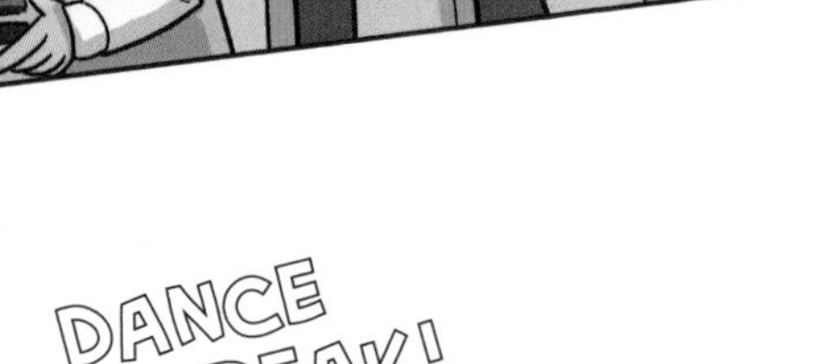
DANCE BREAK!

BEEN GAMING TOO LONG?
JUMP UP AND BOOGIE DOWN
FOR 15 SECONDS.
SHOW OFF YOUR BEST MOVES!

Connect each expression with a line to its meaning.

Peace out	Behind me
Oh snap!	I got you
Hater	Friends
Cha-ching	You've been insulted
Boom	I'm excited
Fired up	Just made money
Up on my back	Goodbye
Homies	Someone who is jealous

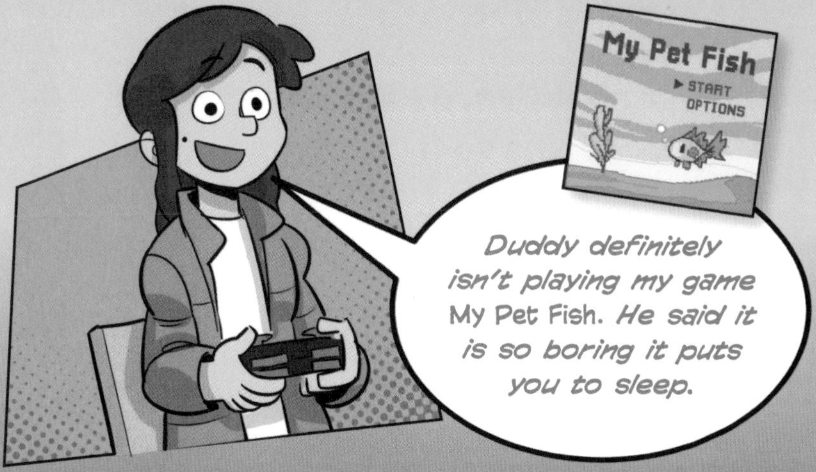
My Pet Fish
▶ START
OPTIONS
Duddy definitely isn't playing my game My Pet Fish. He said it is so boring it puts you to sleep.

Starting with the word **sleep**, draw a line that passes through the fish with words that change only one letter each time to make a new word, ending on the word **dream**. The first one has been done for you.

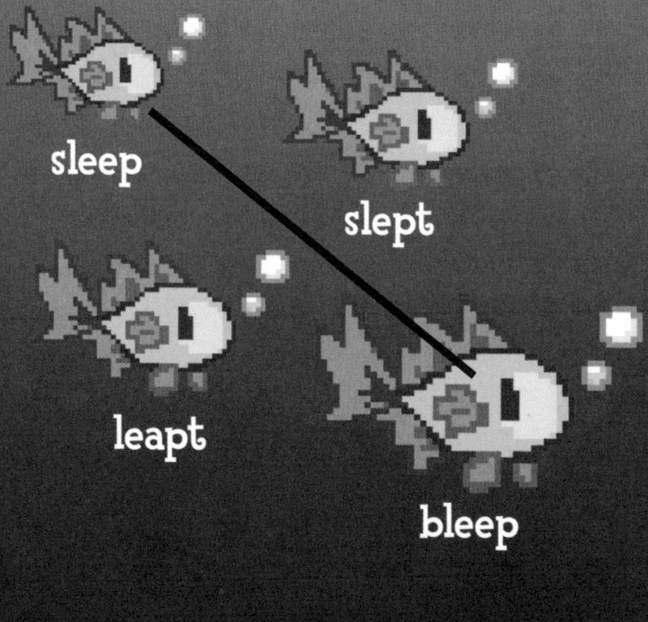
sleep
slept
leapt
bleep

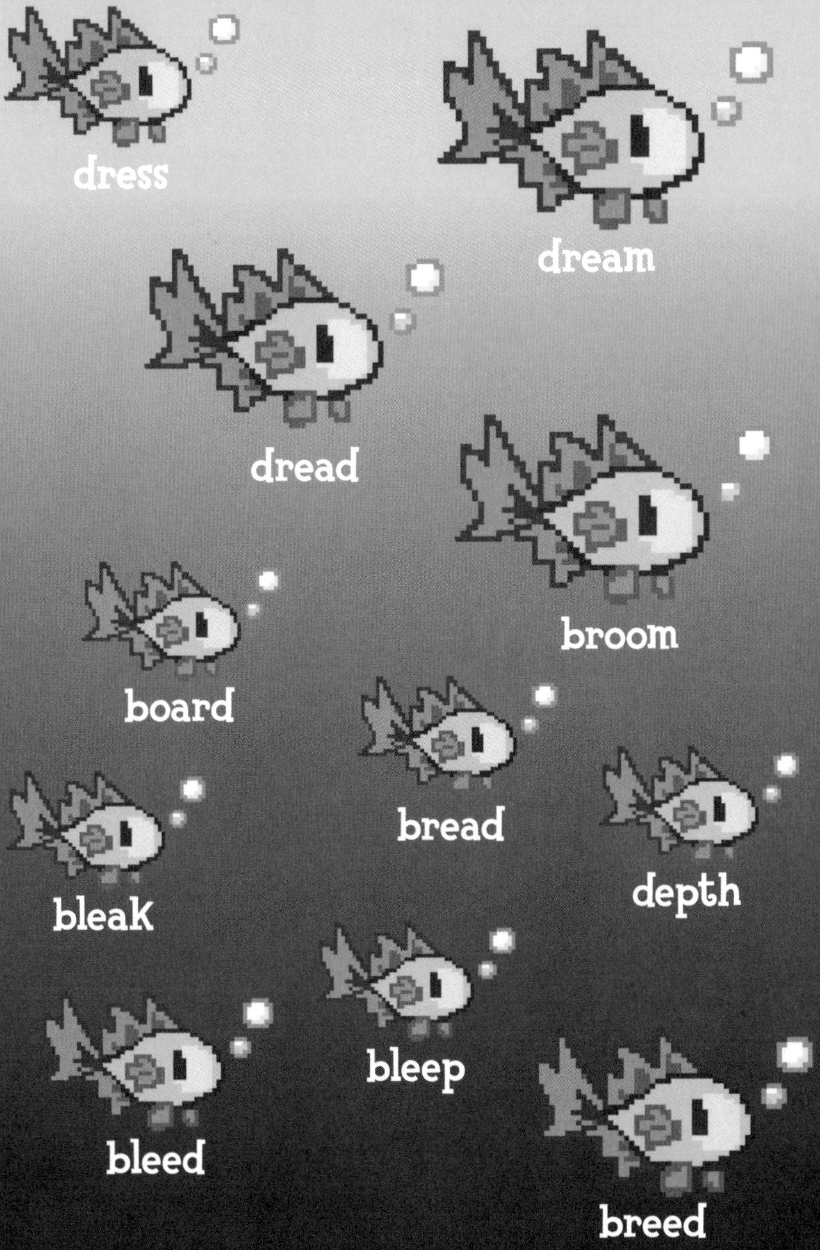
dress
dream
dread
broom
board
bread
bleak
depth
bleep
bleed
breed

BESIDES FEEDING YOUR FISH AND CHANGING ITS GRAVEL COLOR, THERE'S NOT MUCH TO DO IN THE GAME.

Fill in the letters next to the images to show what you can't do with your fish.

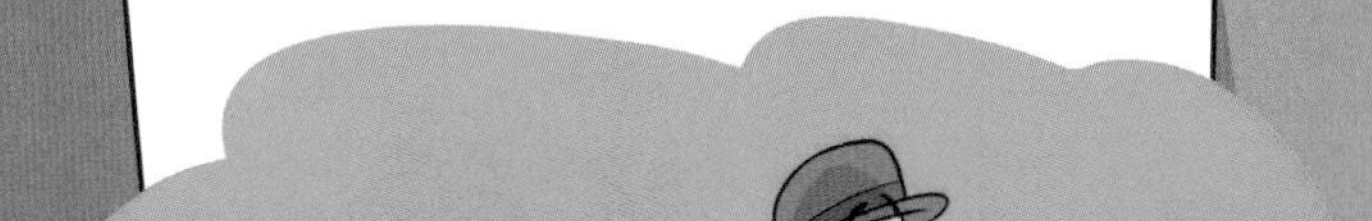

W __ __ __

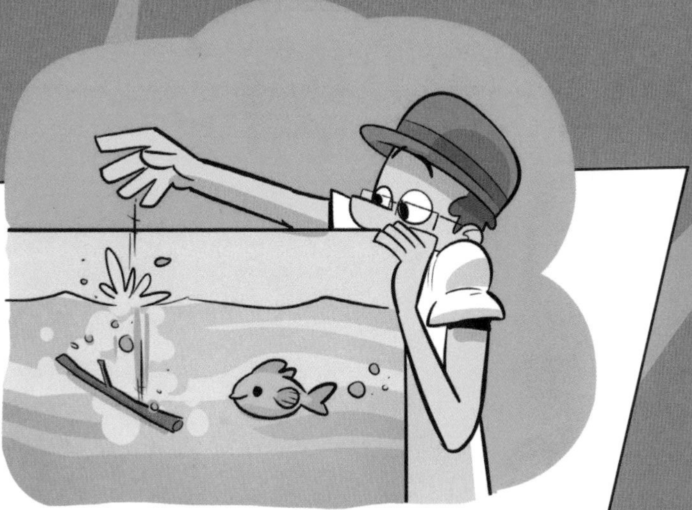

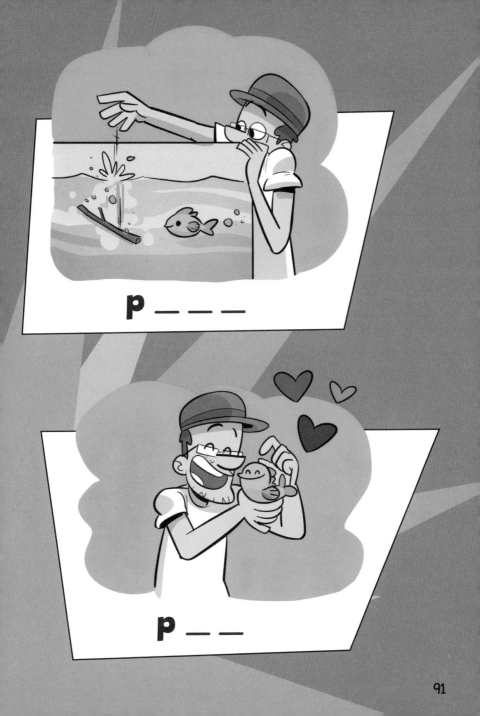

p ___ ___ ___

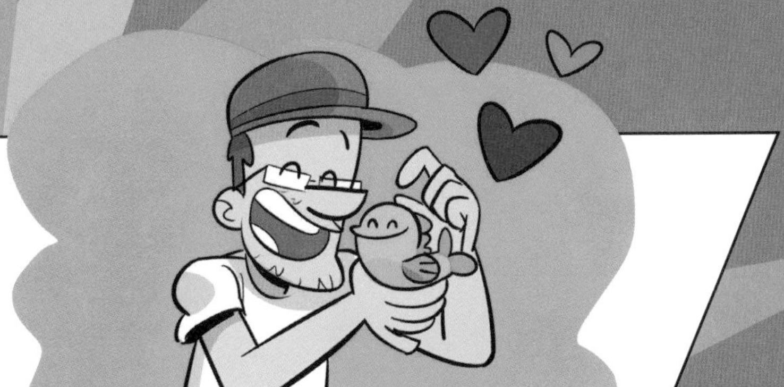

p ___ ___

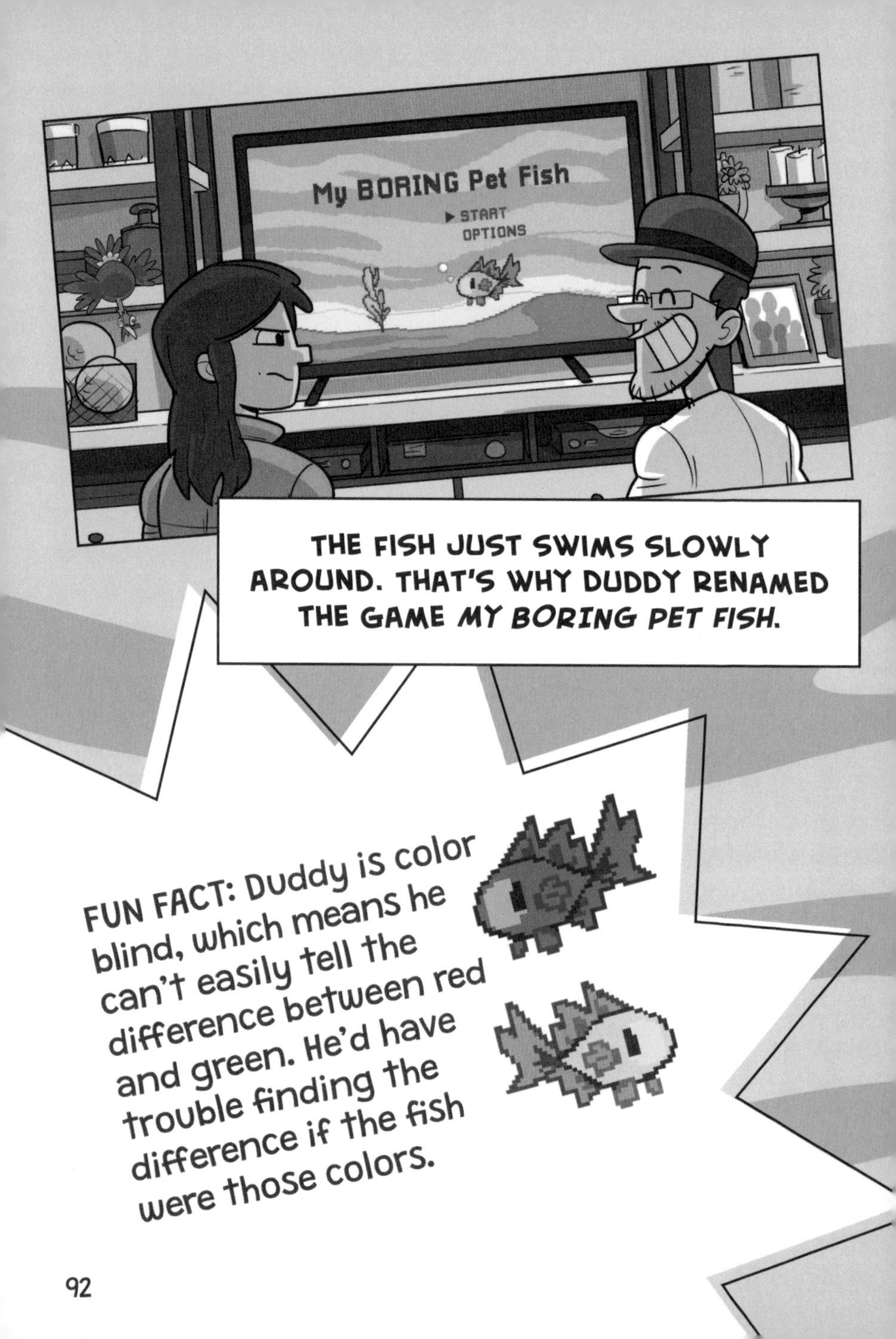
My BORING Pet Fish
▶ START
OPTIONS
THE FISH JUST SWIMS SLOWLY AROUND. THAT'S WHY DUDDY RENAMED THE GAME *MY BORING PET FISH*.
FUN FACT: Duddy is color blind, which means he can't easily tell the difference between red and green. He'd have trouble finding the difference if the fish were those colors.

Can you find and circle the one fish in the tank that isn't bored?

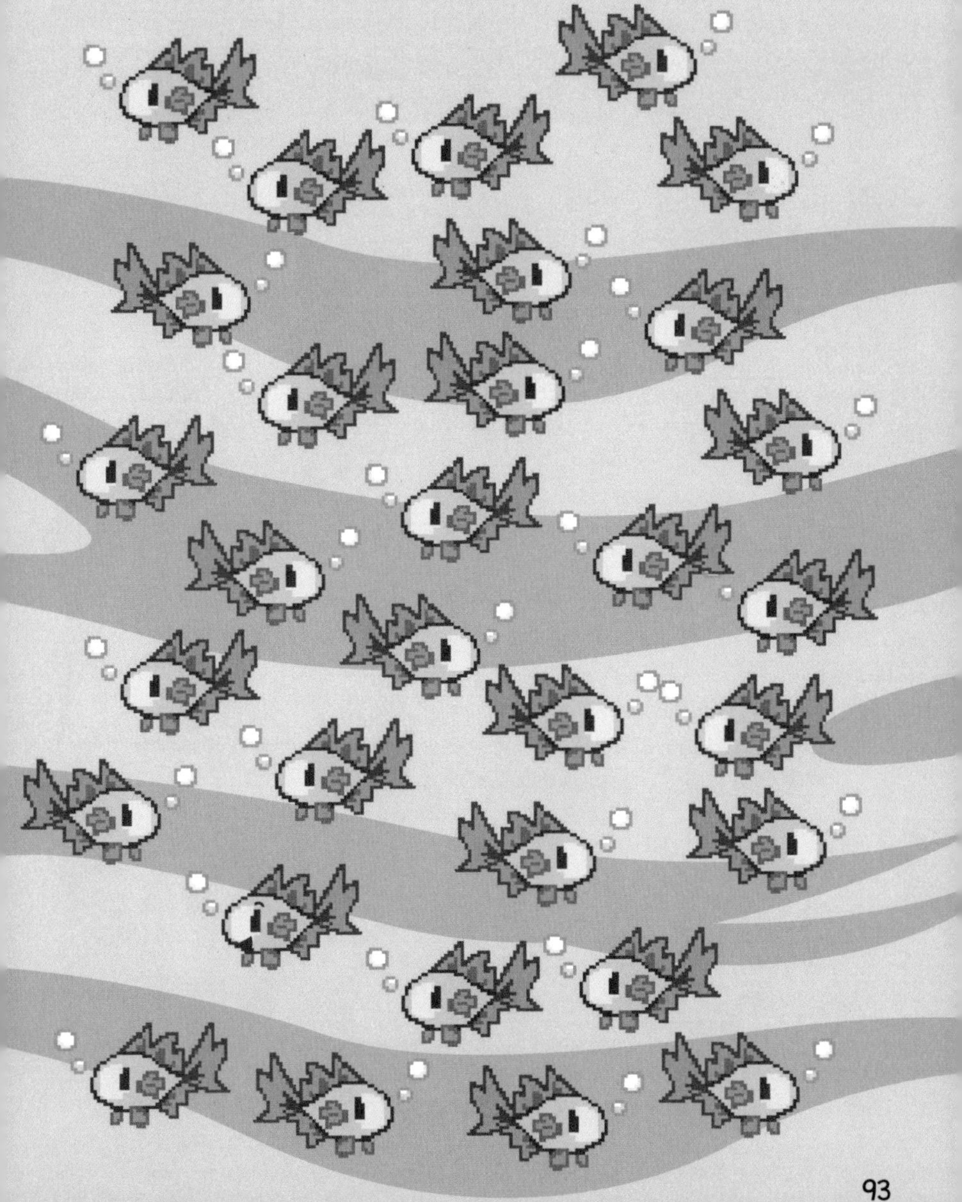

If you were to create a more interesting fish, what would it look like?

DRAW IT HERE.

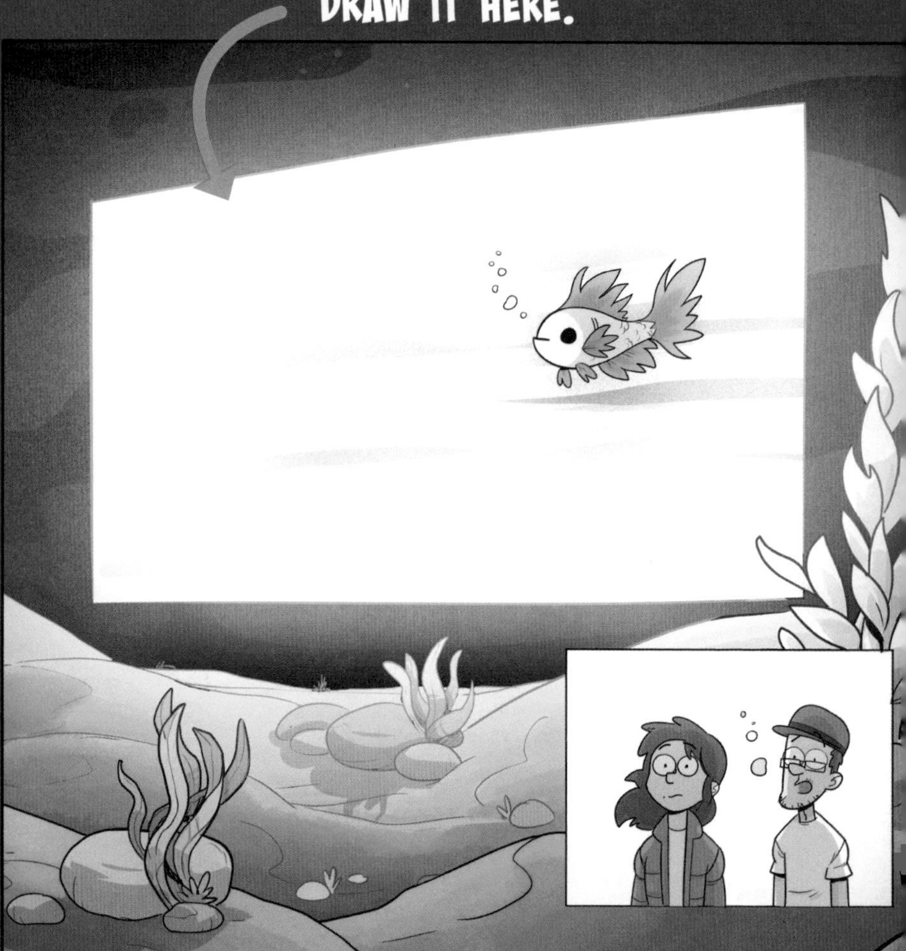

Name your new fish, picking one word from the first column and one from the second.

Captain	Bubbles
Mighty	Squirt
Big	Moby
Tiny	Goldie
Doctor	Coral
Mister	Blue
Lucky	Finn

_____

New fish name

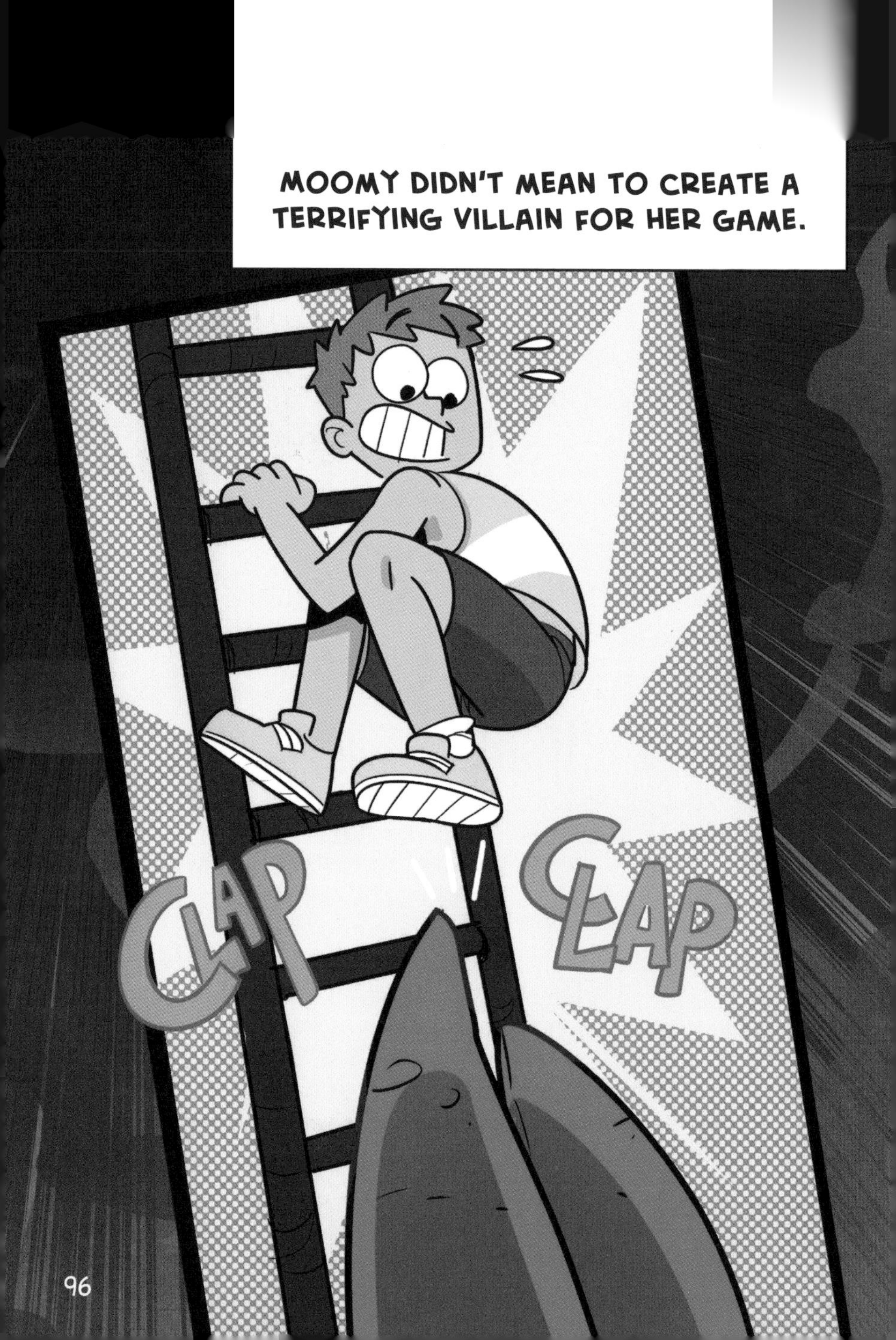
MOOMY DIDN'T MEAN TO CREATE A TERRIFYING VILLAIN FOR HER GAME.
CLAP
CLAP

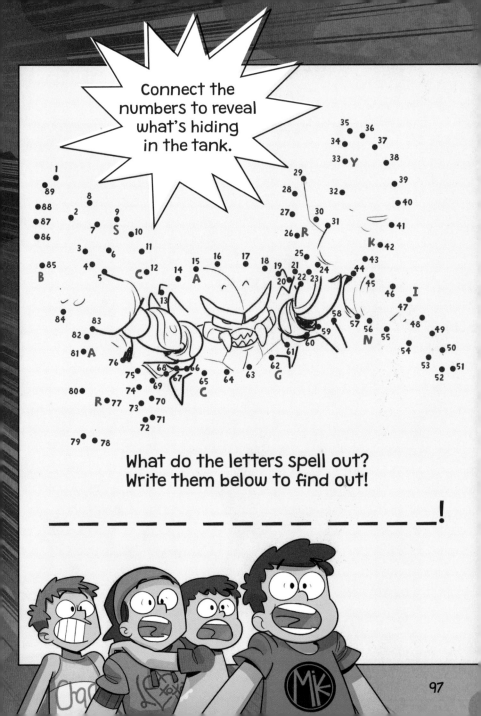

Connect the numbers to reveal what's hiding in the tank.

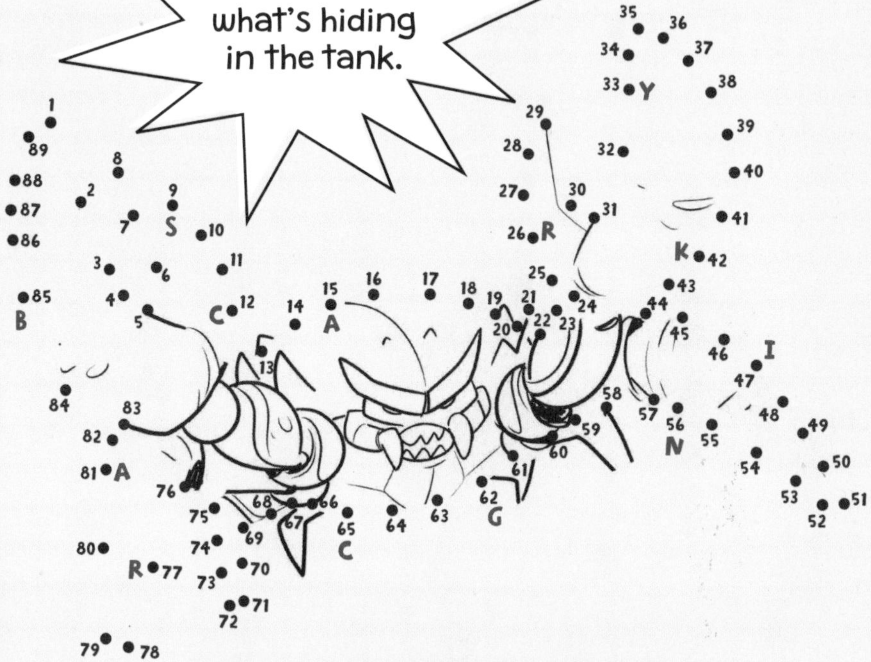

What do the letters spell out?
Write them below to find out!

_ _ _ _ _ _ _ _ _ _ _ _ _ _ _ !

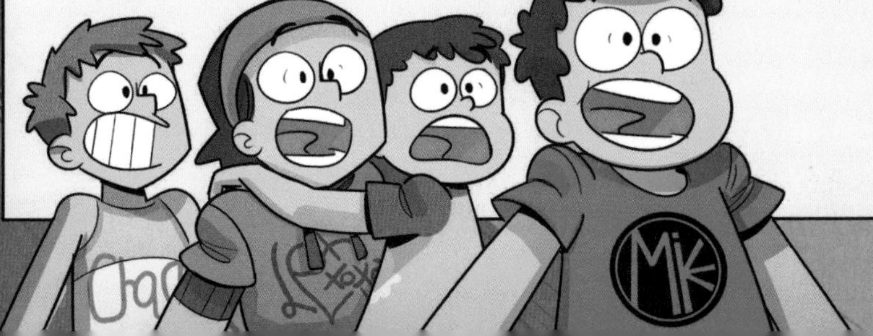

WHAT WOULD YOU DO IF YOU WERE TRAPPED IN AN AQUARIUM?

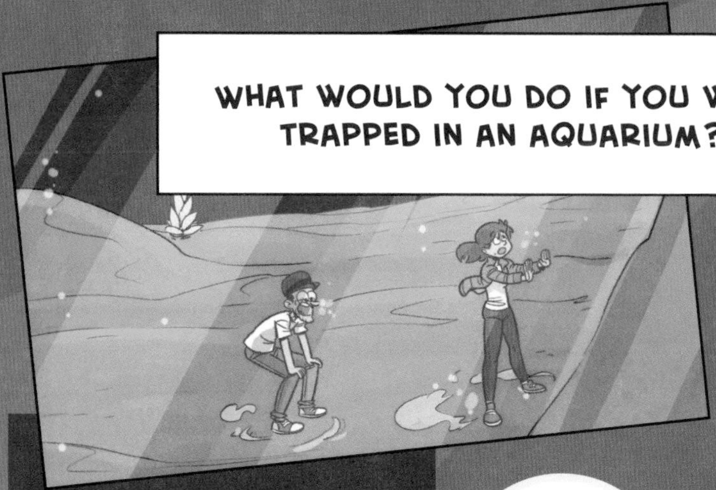

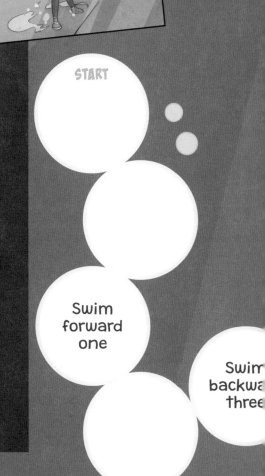

Flip a coin to escape.

Heads = move two spaces forward

Tails = move one space forward

Follow the instructions on the spot where you land.

If it's blank, flip the coin again.

Try to escape in as few coin flips as possible.

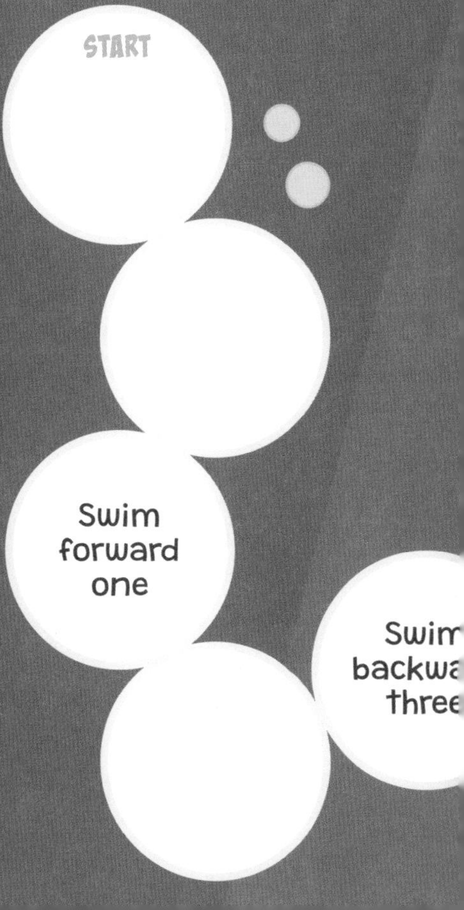
START
Swim forward one

Swim
backward
one

Swim
forward
one

Swim
backward
one

YOU
ESCAPED!

Swim
forward
two

HOW MANY FLIPS DID IT TAKE?

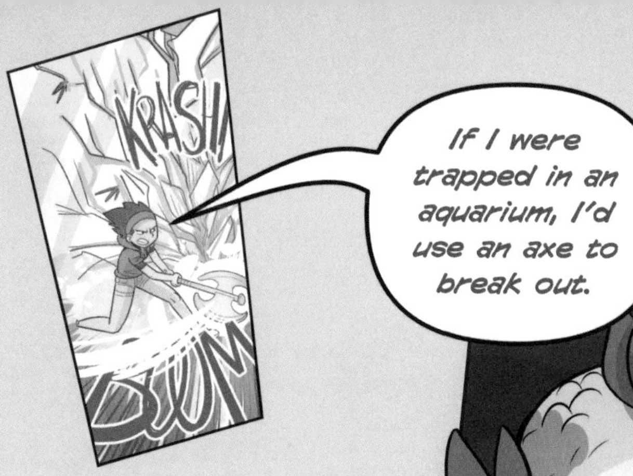
If I were trapped in an aquarium, I'd use an axe to break out.
DUM

It's your turn to be the writer! Fill in the word balloons with what Moomy and Duddy would say as they try to escape the crazy fish and king crab.

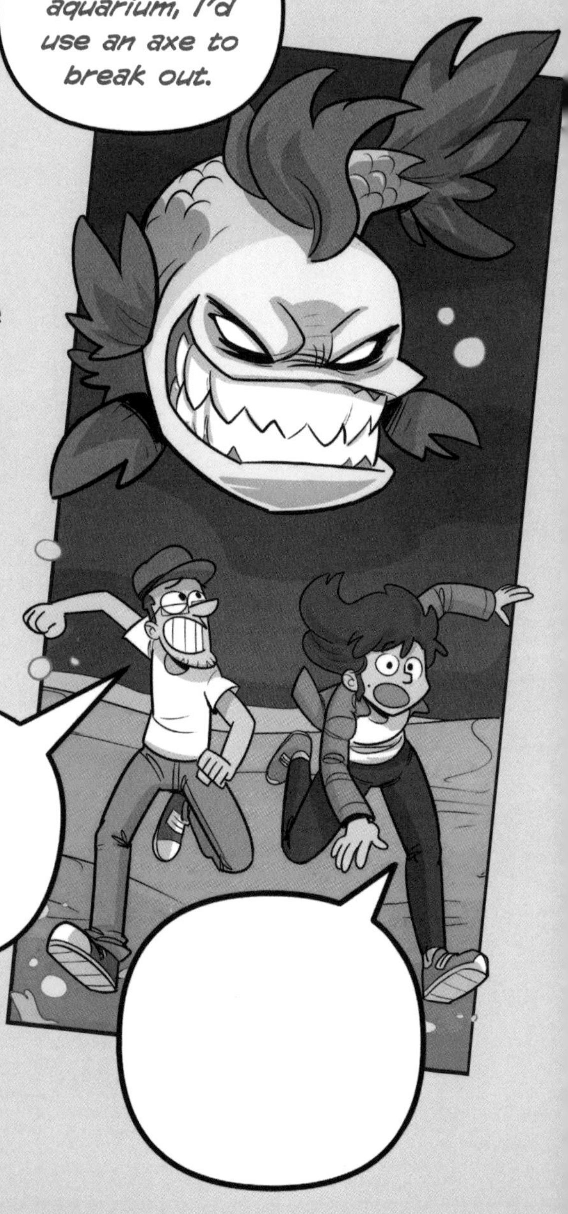

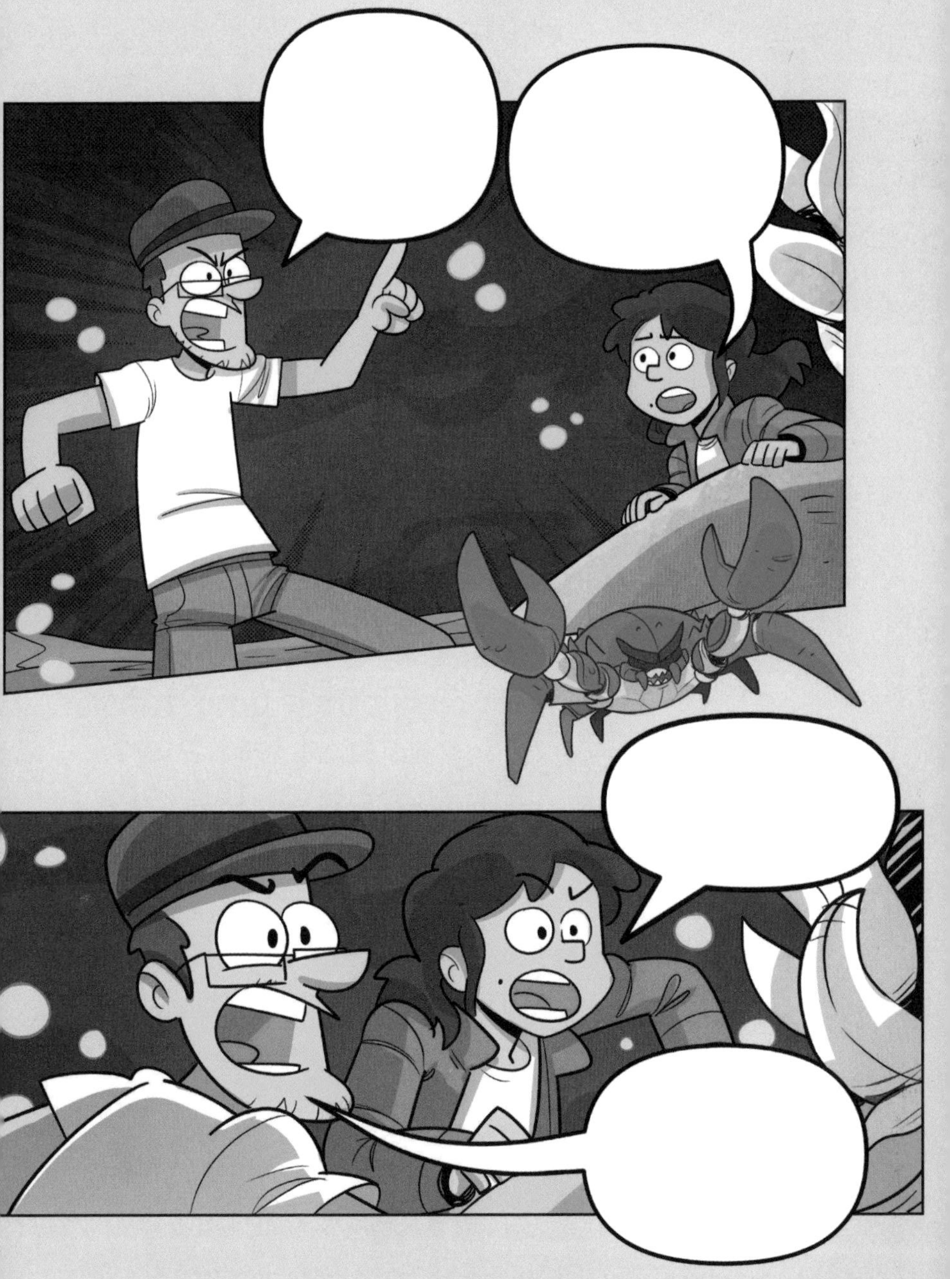

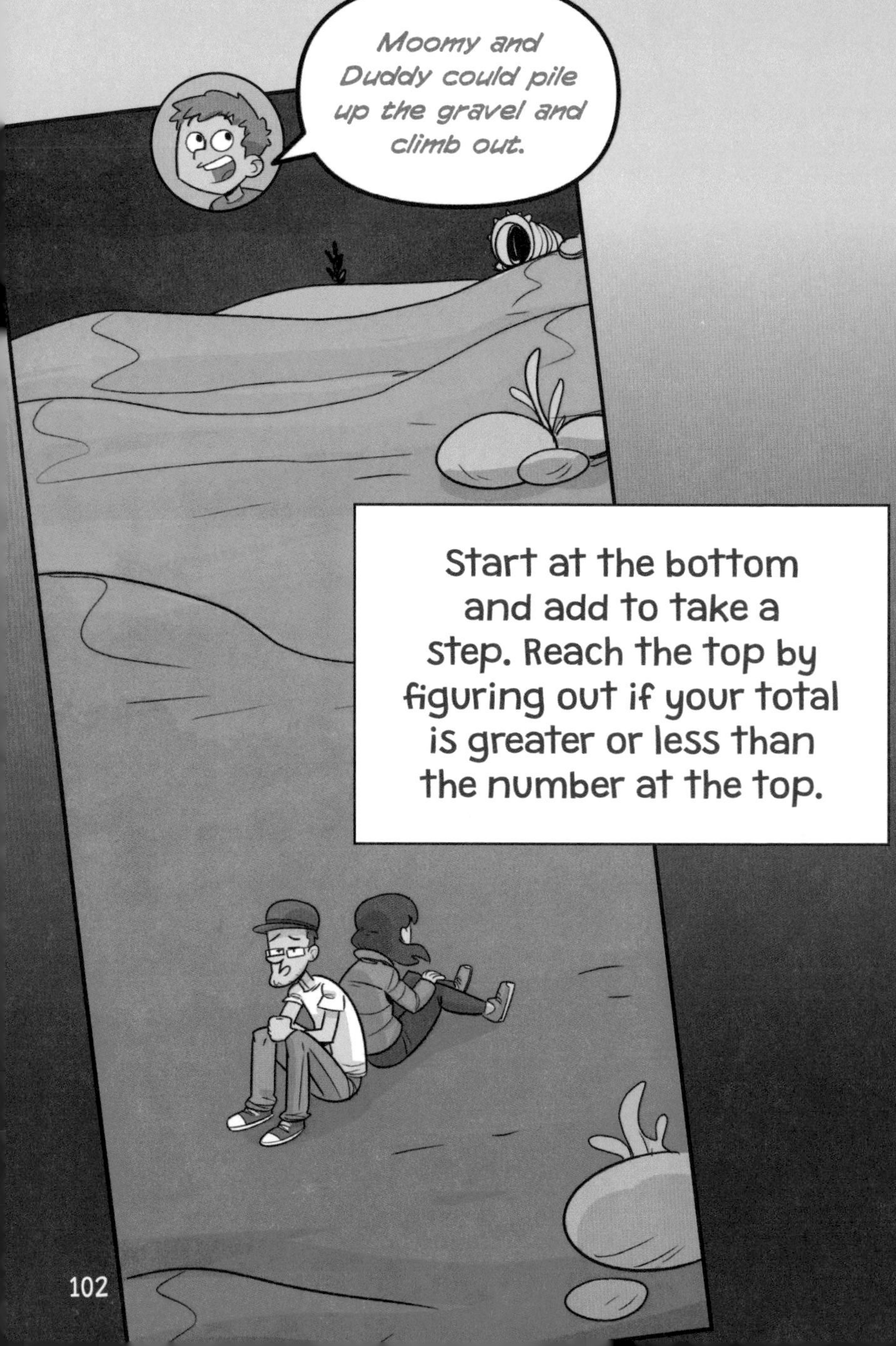
Moomy and Duddy could pile up the gravel and climb out.
Start at the bottom and add to take a step. Reach the top by figuring out if your total is greater or less than the number at the top.

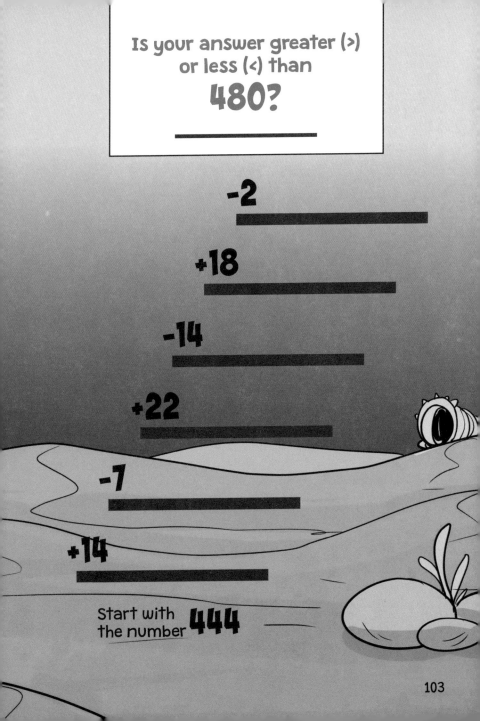

Is your answer greater (>)
or less (<) than
480?

_____

-2

+18

-14

+22

-7

+14

Start with
the number **444**

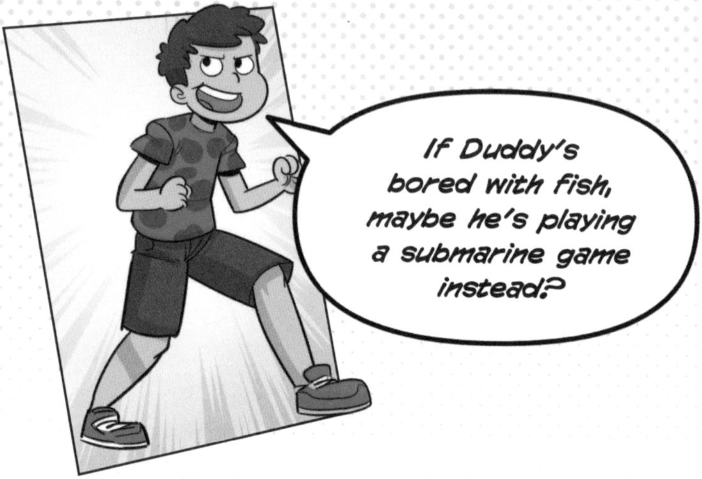
If Duddy's bored with fish, maybe he's playing a submarine game instead?

Starting with the word **SHIP**, create a ladder to escape the submarine using the clues to reach the **NAVY**.

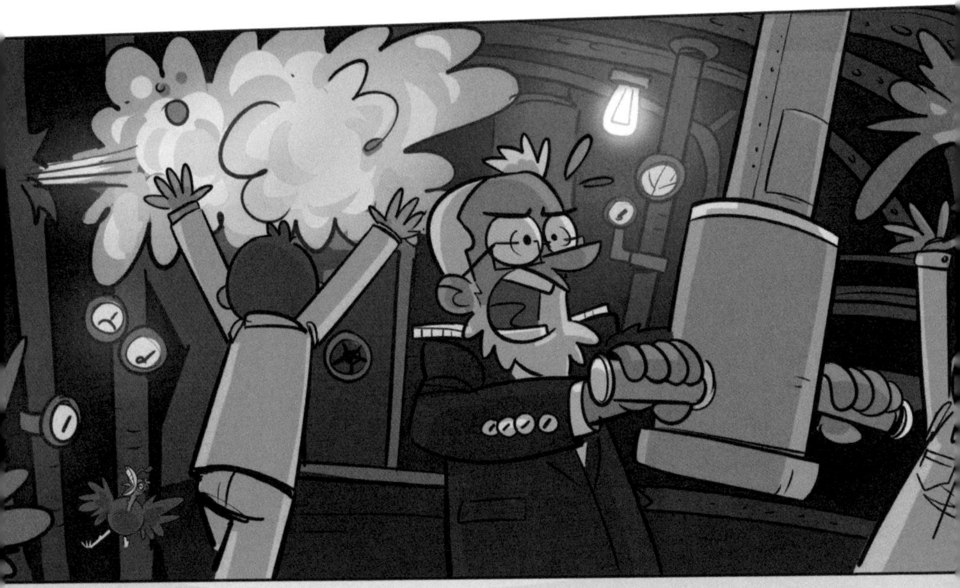

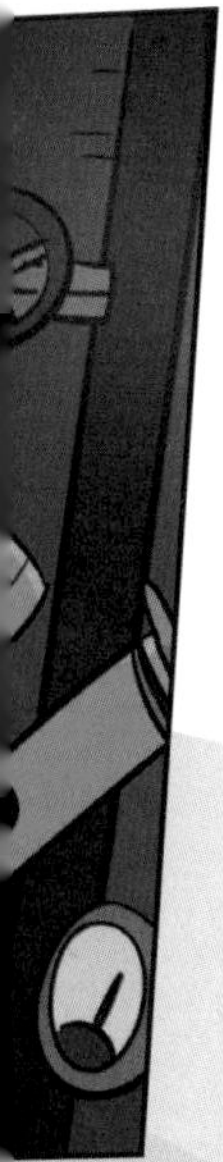

NAVY	take away a letter and change vowels
armed forces at sea	
	take away a letter and change one
a fiction book	
	add a letter to the end
a digging tool	
	change one letter
to push	
	change one letter
remove hair from face	
	change one letter
the form of something	
	add two letters
a guilty feeling	
	change one letter
a meat served with eggs	
	change one letter
male pronoun	
	delete one letter
a body part	
SHIP	
starting word	

Or maybe Duddy is playing a boxing game?

Find the answer to each problem on the right. Then look at the key below to find the letter that corresponds to each answer. The phrase revealed will be the sound of Duddy getting punched.

W = 213

O = 145

P = 265

C = 99

U = 278

H = 58

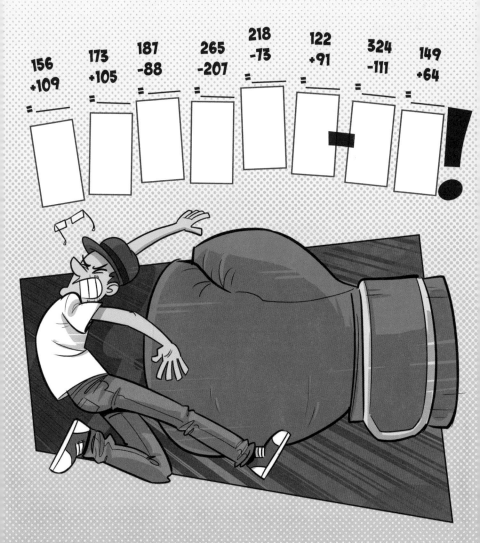

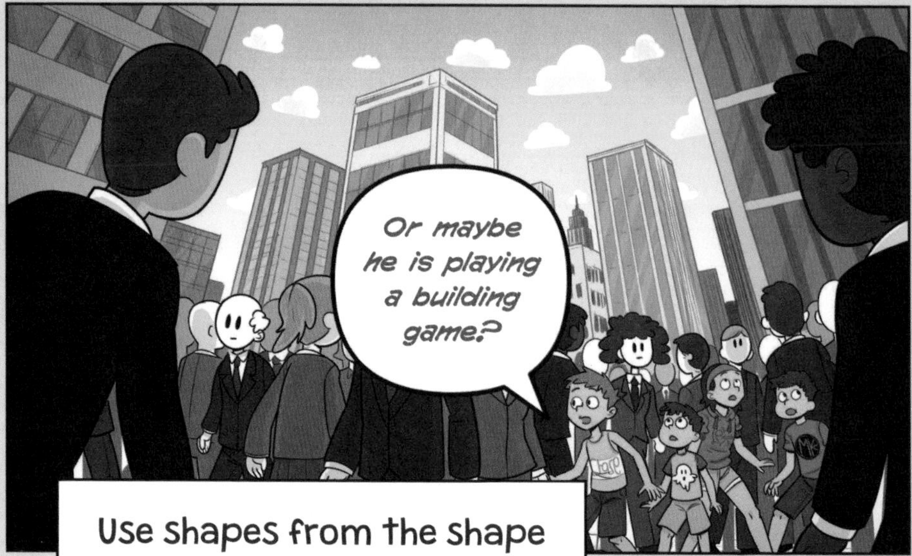
Or maybe he is playing a building game?

Use shapes from the shape bank on the next page to draw your own city.

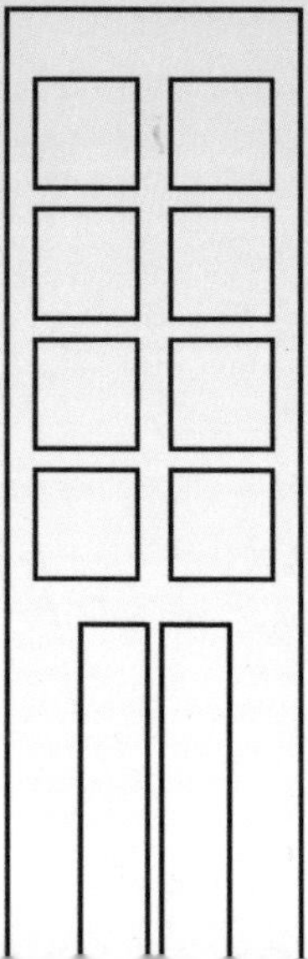

SHAPE BANK

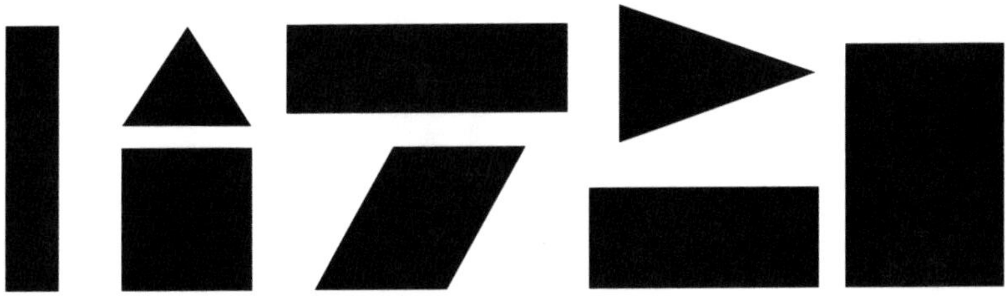

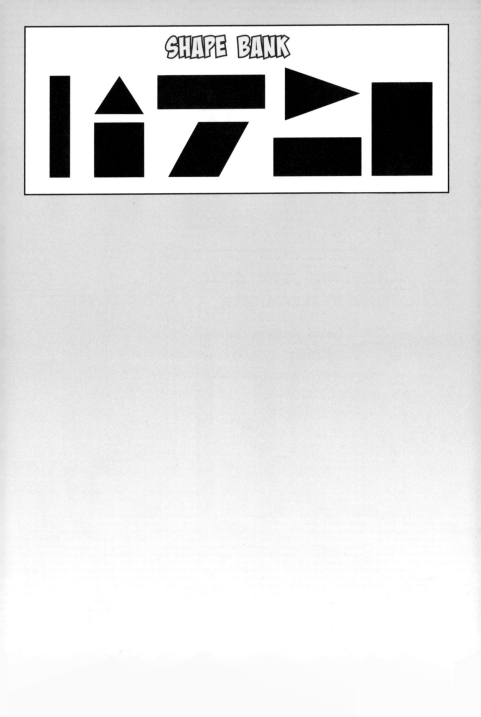

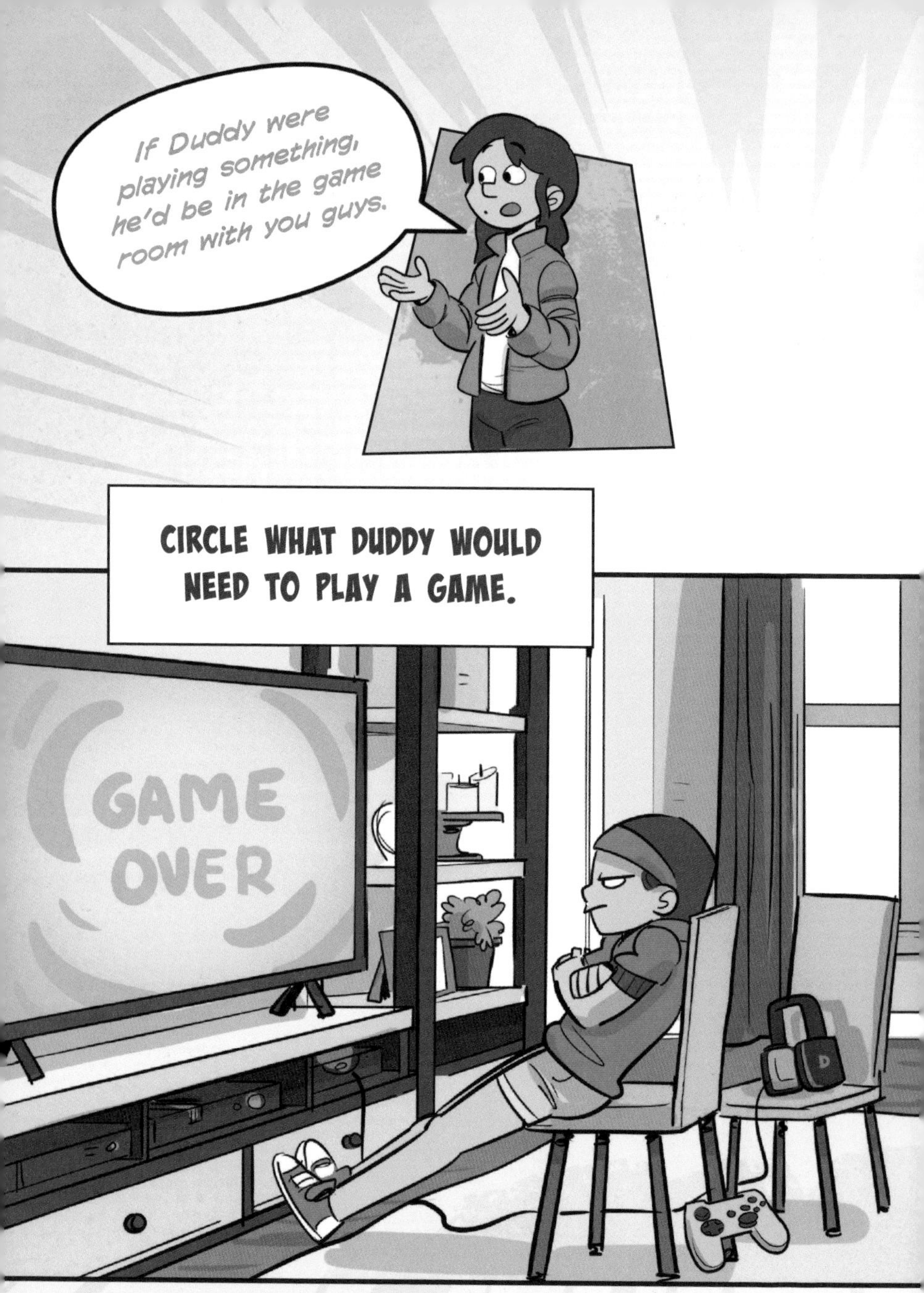
If Duddy were playing something, he'd be in the game room with you guys.
CIRCLE WHAT DUDDY WOULD NEED TO PLAY A GAME.
GAME OVER
D

Design the ultimate controller for your game, assigning a command for each button.

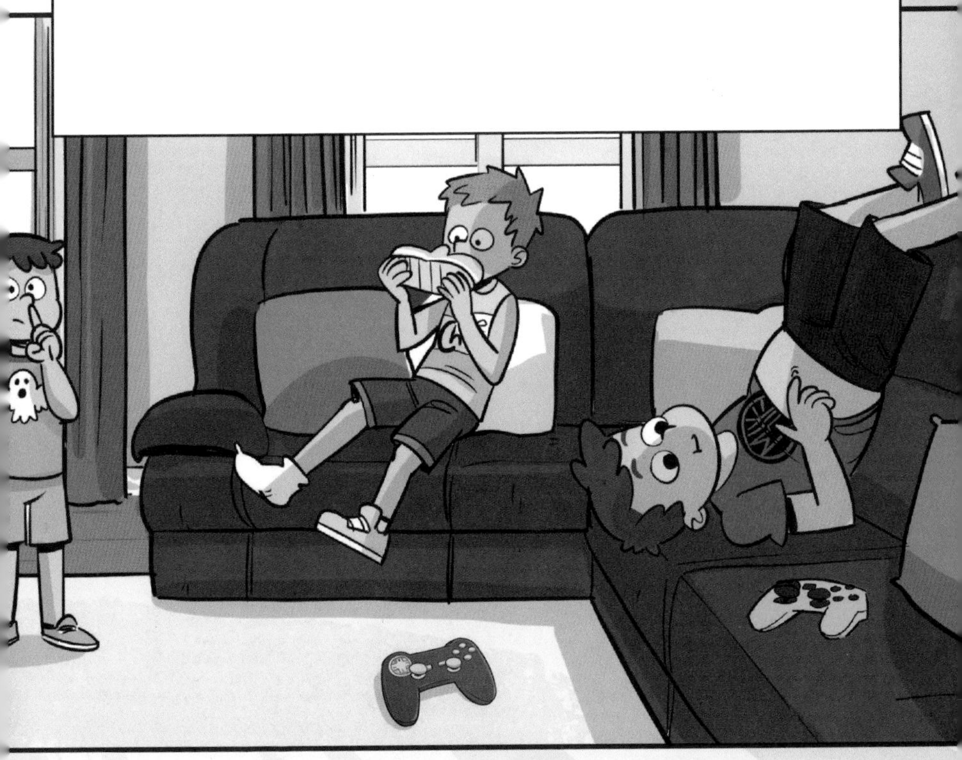

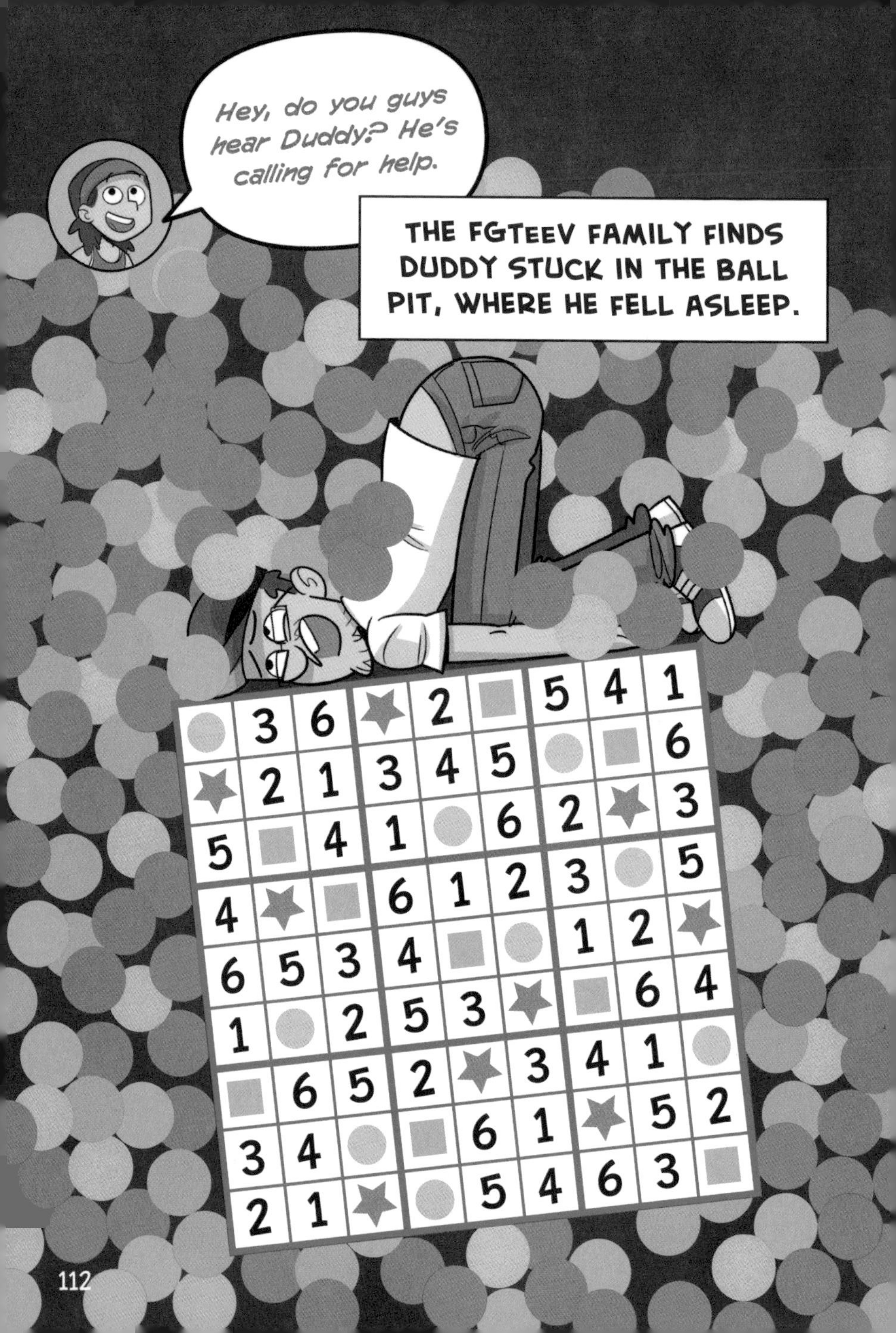
Hey, do you guys hear Duddy? He's calling for help.
THE FGTEEV FAMILY FINDS DUDDY STUCK IN THE BALL PIT, WHERE HE FELL ASLEEP.

●	3	6	★	2	■	5	4	1
★	2	1	3	4	5	●	■	6
5	■	4	1	●	6	2	★	3
4	★	■	6	1	2	3	●	5
6	5	3	4	■	●	1	2	★
1	●	2	5	3	★	■	6	4
■	6	5	2	★	3	4	1	●
3	4	●	■	6	1	★	5	2
2	1	★	●	5	4	6	3	■

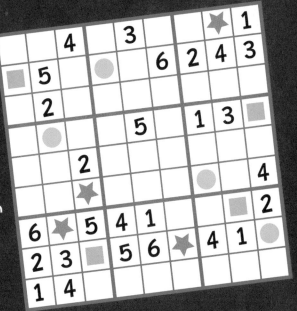

Help him get out by filling in the empty squares with the numbers 1–6 and shapes.

But be sure to use each of them just once in each row and in each column.

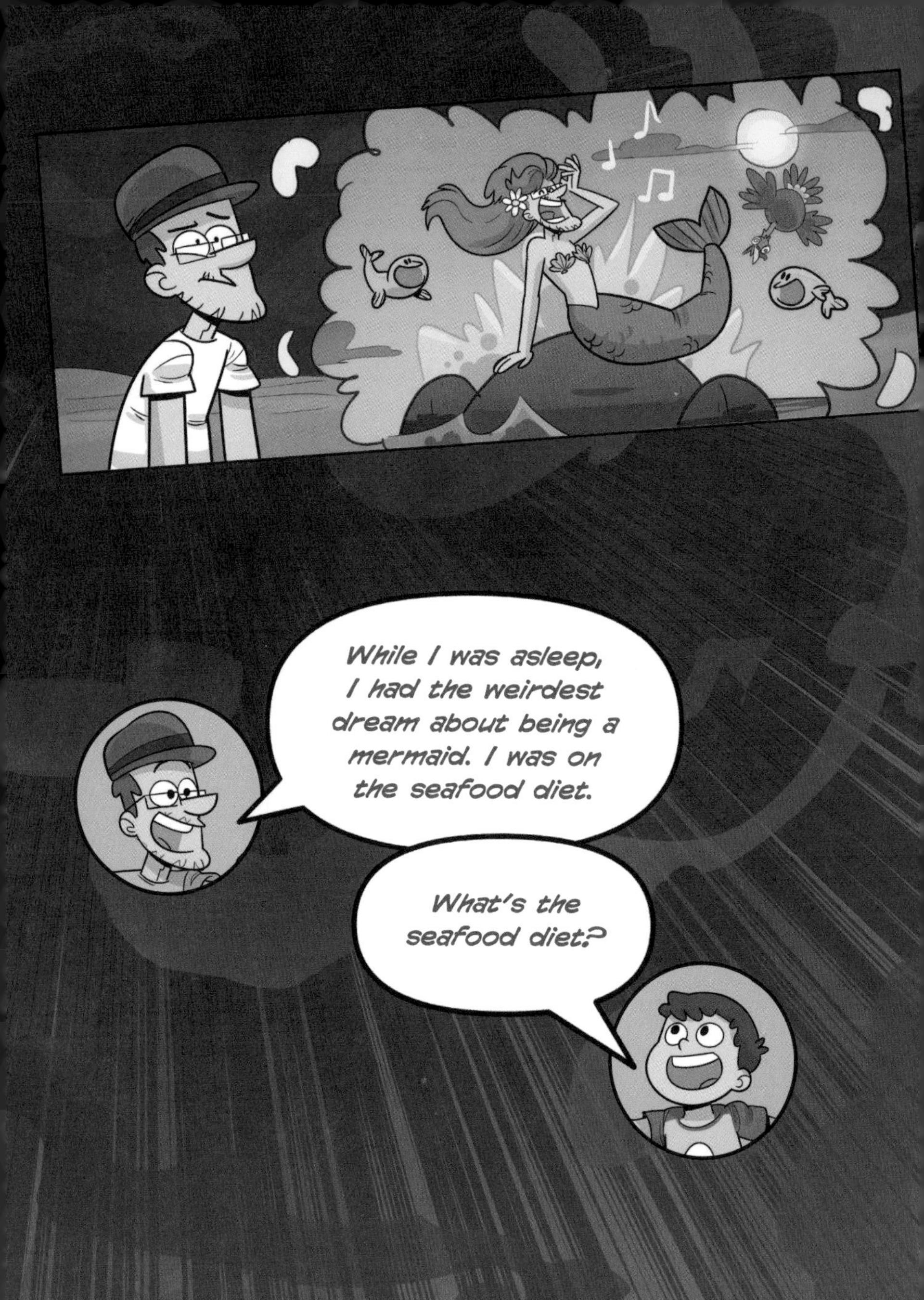

While I was asleep, I had the weirdest dream about being a mermaid. I was on the seafood diet.
What's the seafood diet?

Use the key below to find the answer.

A = Z	J = Q	S = H
B = Y	K = P	T = G
C = X	L = O	U = F
D = W	M = N	V = E
E = V	N = M	W = D
F = U	O = L	X = C
G = T	P = K	Y = B
H = S	Q = J	Z = A
I = R	R = I	

___ ___ ___ ___
R   H V V

___ ___ ___ ___   ___ ___ ___
U L L W   Z M W

___   ___ ___ ___   ___ ___.
R   V Z G   R G

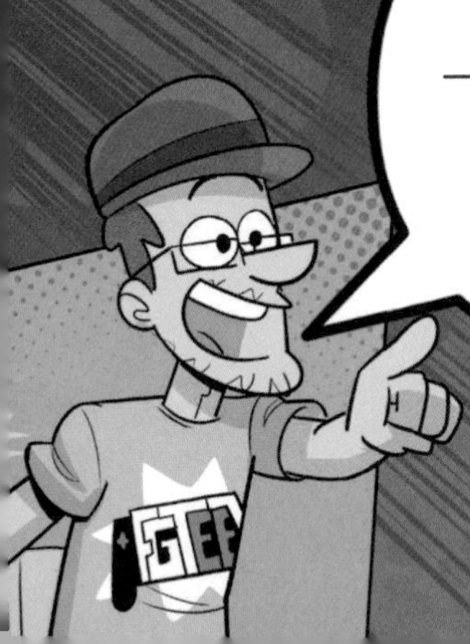

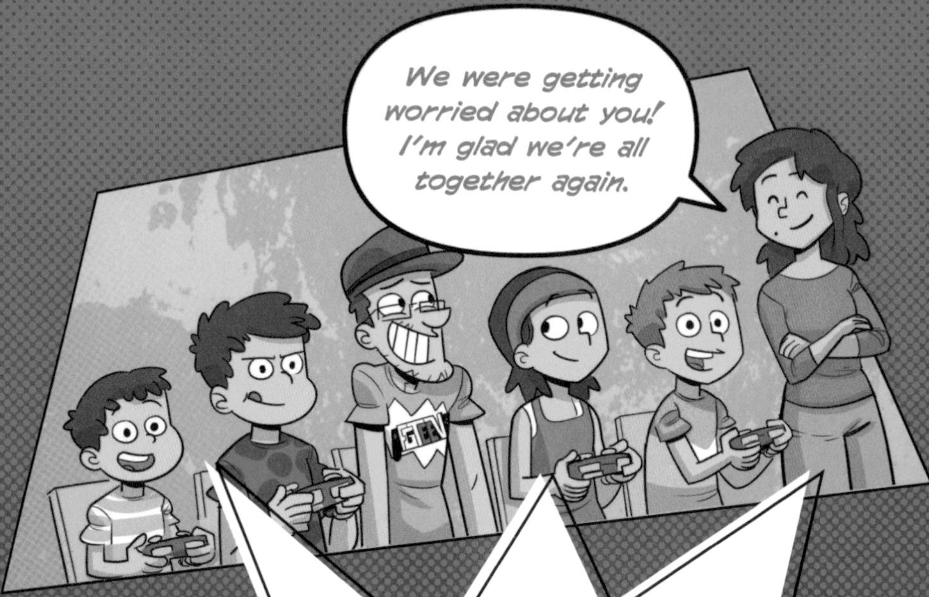

We were getting worried about you! I'm glad we're all together again.

FIND WHAT THE FAMILY LIKES TO DO TOGETHER IN THE WORD SEARCH ON THE RIGHT.

game	joke
rap	read comics
eat	hang out
laugh	watch movies
play	dance

P	E	R	V	W	D	A	N	C	E	Y
X	T	N	X	P	A	R	P	G	L	W
S	E	I	V	O	M	H	C	T	A	W
G	C	N	D	D	B	J	L	U	B	J
Q	A	I	D	X	O	H	U	O	J	K
P	X	M	M	K	J	V	D	G	X	N
F	P	S	E	O	H	D	D	N	Q	Z
F	L	R	T	G	C	R	H	A	E	Q
J	A	J	U	S	Y	D	Z	H	E	M
C	Y	A	Z	A	Y	B	A	L	Z	B
W	L	V	M	T	Z	C	M	E	V	B
U	X	H	V	I	A	U	E	O	R	E
S	M	R	V	U	K	E	X	J	R	K

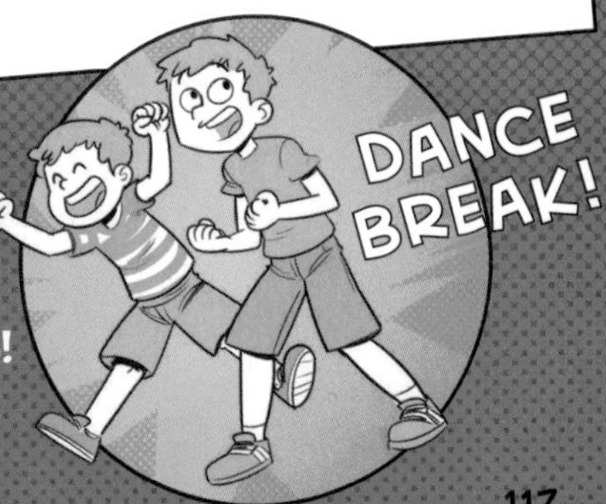
DANCE BREAK!

BEEN GAMING TOO LONG? JUMP UP AND BOOGIE DOWN FOR 15 SECONDS. SHOW OFF YOUR BEST MOVES!

ACROSS

1. Favorite of old people
2. Kid boss
3. Middle boy
4. Frightened fowl
5. OB (oldest boy)
6. Fun-loving rapper
7. Best dog ever

DOWN

6. Rap about laser gun sound
8. Woman in charge

HOW WELL DO YOU NOW KNOW THE FGTEEV FAMILY? FILL IN THE CROSSWORD BELOW AND SEE.

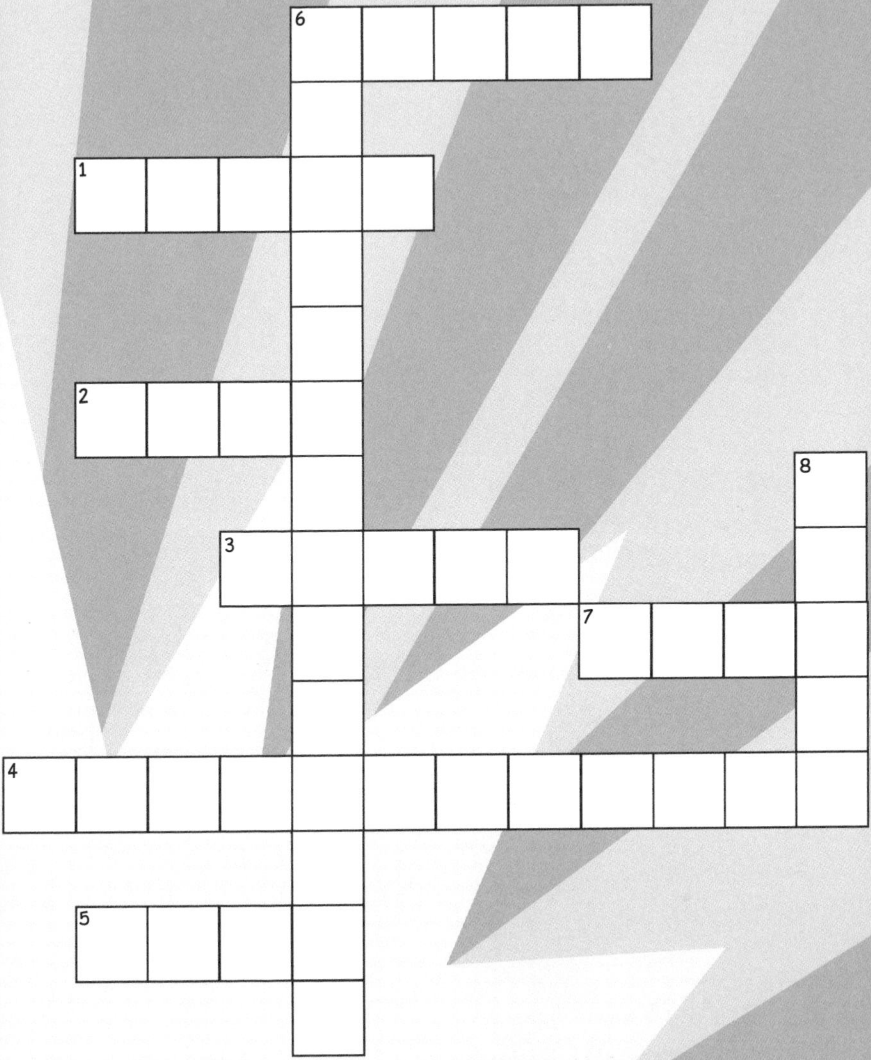
6
1
2
8
3
7
4
5

ANSWER KEY

Page 2

P Q V B S Y Z R G P R X N W
W A D J G B P J O K Y O O A
G W N Q G M N A F H C M X F
D N X C E K T L O A N X H F
H U Y L A M V W B Q W X I L
H B C O E K K Y Q Y M L F E
M O R A N G E J U I C E O S
J X L Z M K A S O V B B V N
V L W W R L S B Z E Y J W J
E K S U U B P V U F S Z B P
L M T S O G G Z D P H B O J
E F Z P B L A E R E C Z P L

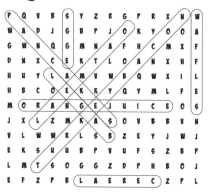

Page 3

gummy bears
cheese balls
hot sauce
pickles

Page 4

Duddy
Lexo
Mikester
Moomz

Page 5

Page 6

welcoming
safe
friendly
cozy
peaceful
normal
pretty

Page 11

Page 17

1 SPEAR
2 CANNON
3 GRENADE
4 AX
5 KNIFE
6 BOMB
GUN

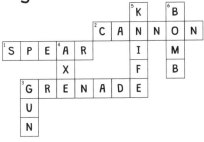

Page 19

Answer to joke:
Oreo rolling down a hill.

Page 21

5 x 9 =
53 - 16 =
8 x 9 =
16 + 15 =
37
45
72
31

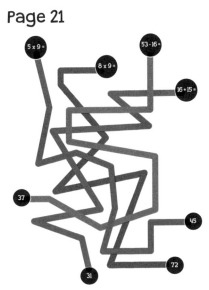

Pages 22–23

line, fine, five, dive,
live, like, lake, cake,
cape, tape

Page 25

Who's a good girl?

Page 27

V	I	P	N	Z	P	X	S	K	V	P	X	U	H
W	Z	D	B	R	P	K	I	W	U	F	F	O	C
G	R	D	I	S	G	U	S	T	I	N	G	D	Y
G	U	E	U	I	T	D	R	J	Z	U	M	O	T
S	G	W	T	T	X	I	G	J	D	F	X	R	R
M	S	N	E	C	D	N	E	T	T	O	R	O	I
G	E	O	P	S	H	K	T	Y	R	U	V	U	D
J	V	K	R	Y	D	E	D	S	M	Z	Z	S	J
D	O	T	T	G	R	R	D	Y	Y	K	T	X	S
L	A	S	H	B	X	Z	M	L	C	Z	B	G	E
C	A	P	Q	P	F	E	I	C	K	Y	I	A	I
N	B	U	C	M	M	D	Q	P	G	X	N	M	D

Page 29

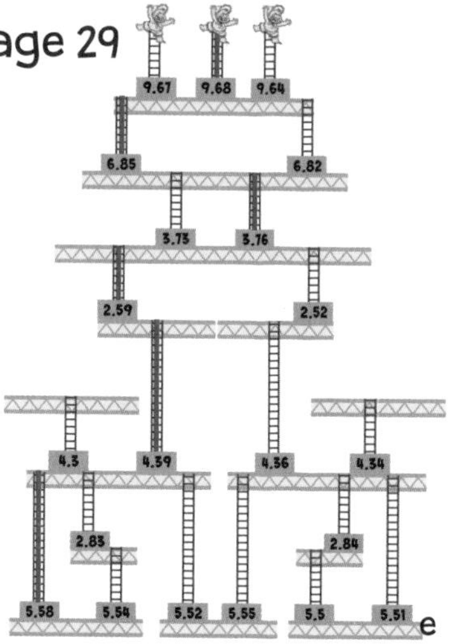

9.67
9.68
9.64
6.85
6.82
3.73
3.76
2.59
2.52
4.3
4.39
4.36
4.34
2.83
2.84
5.58
5.54
5.52
5.55
5.5
5.51

Page 31

box of rocks — Caveman Carl
hissing vipers — Lord Snake Pit
feather pillow — Super Soft Sally
pail of slop — Sooey Pig
rotten eggs — Cluck Cluck Buck

Page 37

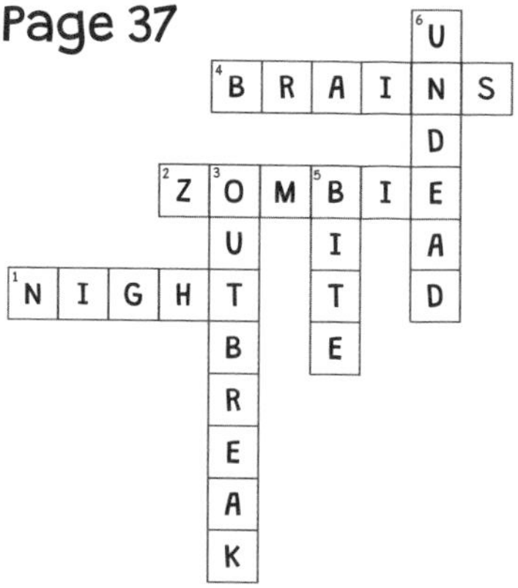

1 NIGHT
2 ZOMBIE
3 OUTBREAK
4 BRAINS
5 BITE
6 UNDEAD

Pages 40–41

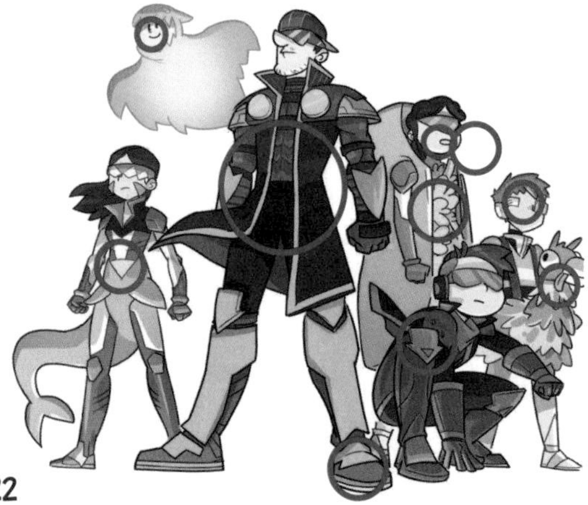

Page 43

Hide and Shriek!

Page 46

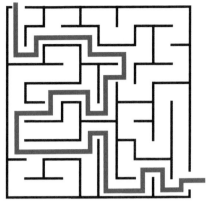

Page 47

Page 49

O	Z	G	H	H	P	E	K	H	V	U
K	X	K	C	O	Y	L	R	C	C	C
K	V	N	H	F	A	T	N	C	I	J
W	U	S	H	O	O	T	U	A	U	K
P	I	I	S	B	M	A	R	M	A	K
Z	C	J	F	L	L	B	P	O	G	R
B	E	A	C	E	F	S	E	D	I	H
P	H	P	U	L	K	D	R	B	Q	Z
L	X	U	A	N	O	G	N	L	W	J
O	K	D	G	C	G	N	S	A	M	Q
W	P	B	N	S	S	X	E	S	X	B
F	E	W	Y	M	Z	E	X	T	Q	C
P	U	R	E	W	O	P	I	M	C	F
O	H	S	Y	F	C	F	V	L	C	L
S	K	I	O	Y	C	J	I	L	K	E
Z	O	H	L	S	Q	G	B	K	I	I

Page 51

transforming
fighting
chilling

Page 53

He's right **behind** me.
He's gonna **find** me.
I've gotta **run**.
This ain't no **fun**.
Boom bash **crash**
I've gotta **dash**.

Page 57

playe = play
promese = promise
skool = school
mite = might
exsited = excited

Page 59

The most you can get is 12.

Page 61

I	H	K	L	F	X	S	T	X	O	A	S
C	L	H	C	R	Q	L	L	D	C	Q	R
E	B	C	U	E	V	J	A	T	G	N	E
C	Q	T	R	N	C	H	W	M	P	G	G
R	E	K	A	C	L	E	N	N	U	F	R
E	P	V	I	H	Y	E	C	M	B	I	U
A	O	P	X	F	P	V	M	X	T	D	B
M	E	C	W	R	K	Y	D	T	X	C	M
T	Z	Y	S	I	B	C	E	Q	F	I	A
B	L	V	P	E	I	H	T	W	X	H	H
P	R	Y	A	S	G	J	Z	K	O	H	I
O	I	R	B	A	J	N	R	R	U	W	I
W	S	Z	P	S	L	U	S	H	I	E	X
P	D	S	Z	X	V	C	D	Q	R	L	M
R	O	A	I	A	Q	K	M	Y	T	J	B

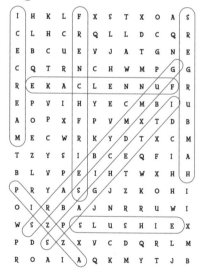

Page 62

Page 63

$28.80

Pages 64–65

darling
precious
adorable
dear

Page 67

5, 13, 21, 29, 37, 45
1, 3, 9, 27, 81
22, 29, 36, 43, 50
16, 13, 10, 7, 4
2, 4, 8, 16, 32

Page 69

3	1	5	4	●	2	■	6	★
4	■	2	★	6	5	1	3	●
6	★	●	1	■	3	2	4	5
★	2	3	■	1	6	5	●	4
■	6	4	2	5	●	★	1	3
5	●	1	3	★	4	6	■	2
●	5	★	6	3	1	4	2	■
2	3	6	5	4	■	●	★	1
1	4	■	●	2	★	3	5	6

4	3	■	2	6	★	●	1	5
6	●	★	4	5	1	2	3	■
1	5	2	■	3	●	★	4	6
●	■	4	3	1	2	6	5	★
★	1	5	6	4	■	3	●	2
3	2	6	★	●	5	1	■	4
5	★	3	●	■	6	4	2	1
2	4	1	5	★	3	■	6	●
■	6	●	1	2	4	5	★	3

Page 70

They are all odd numbers.

Page 71

Game time is family time

Page 78

Page 81

Page 83

blam
bang
pow
wham
ka-boom
crack

Page 85

robber
copper
you
got you
pew
too

125

Page 87

Peace out = Goodbye

Oh snap! = You've been insulted

Hater = Someone who is jealous

Cha-ching = Just made money

Boom = I got you

Fired up = I'm excited

Up on my back = Behind me

Homies = Friends

Pages 88–89

sleep, bleep, bleed, breed, bread, dread, dream.

Pages 90–91

walk
play
pet

Page 93

Page 97

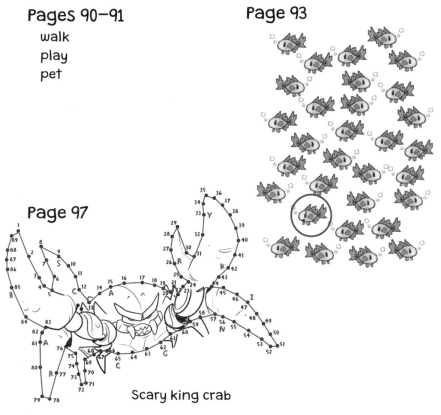

Scary king crab

Page 103

LESS THAN 480

-2	475
+18	477
-14	459
+22	473
-7	451
+14	458

Page 105

ship, hip, him, ham,
shame, shape, shave,
shove, shovel, novel, navy

Page 107

PUCHOW-WW!

Pages 110–111

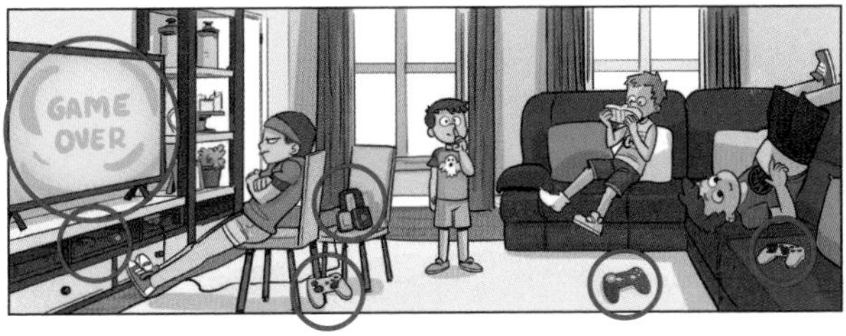

GAME OVER

Page 113

●	6	4	2	3	5	■	★	1
■	5	1	●	★	6	2	4	3
★	2	3	■	4	1	6	●	5
4	●	6	★	5	2	1	3	■
3	■	2	1	●	4	★	5	6
5	1	★	6	■	3	●	2	4
6	★	5	4	1	●		■	2
2	3	■	5	6	★	4	1	●
1	4	●	3	2	■	5	6	★

3	6	5	■	●	★	2	4	1
●	4	★	2	1	6	3	■	5
2	■	1	5	4	3	★	●	6
4	5	6	★	2	●	1	3	■
■	★	●	3	6	1	4	5	2
1	3	2	4	■	5	6	★	●
★	1	3	●	5	2	■	6	4
6	●	4	1	3	■	5	2	★
5	2	■	6	★	4	●	1	3

Page 115

I see food and I eat it.

Page 117

```
P  E  R  V  W  (D  A  N  C  E)  Y
X  T  N  X  (P  A  R)  P  G  L  W
(S  E  I  V  O  M  H  C  (T  A  W)
(G  C  N  D  D  B  J)  L  U  B  J
Q  (A  I  D  X  O  H  U  O  J  K
P  X  M  M  K  J  V  D  G  X  N
F  (P  S  (E  O  H)  D  D  N  Q  Z
F  L  R  T  G  C  R  H  A  E  Q
J  A  J  U  S  Y  D  Z  H  E  M
C  Y  A  Z  A  Y  B  A  L  Z  B
W  (L  V  M  T  Z  C  M  E  V  B
U  X  H  V  I  A  U  E  O  R)  E
S  M  R  V  U  K  E)  X  J  R  K
```

Page 119

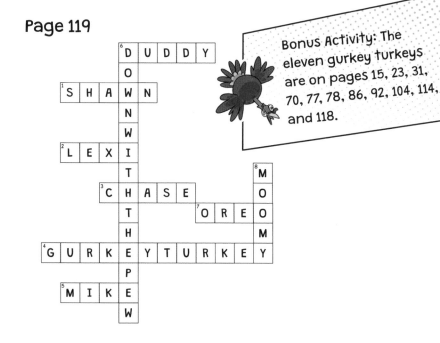

```
         ⁶D  U  D  D  Y
         O
  ¹S  H  A  W  N
         N
         W
  ²L  E  X  I
         T                    ⁸M
      ³C  H  A  S  E          O
         T        ⁷O  R  E  O  O
         H                    M
⁴G  U  R  K  E  Y  T  U  R  K  E  Y
         P
   ⁵M  I  K  E
         W
```

Bonus Activity: The eleven gurkey turkeys are on pages 15, 23, 31, 70, 77, 78, 86, 92, 104, 114, and 118.